Dec 2023

Frani~

All the best for
the coming year!

Bill Anderson

Dec 2023

Tales to Tell

Expressions
Volume XII
2023

Varenna Writers Club
Edited by Susan Bono

Copyright © 2023

Edited by Susan Bono

Book Design by Jennifer March

Cover Design by Sunfield Design

Front Cover Image by Denis Degioanni & Kevin Erdvig

Back Cover Image by Toa Heftiba

ISBN: 9798866537679

The Varenna Writers Club is sponsored by
Varenna at Fountaingrove.

I believe in stories, in their incredible power to keep people alive, to keep the living alive, and the dead.
Tim O'Brien

Contents

Bill Ardizoia

Rugger 24

Oh . . . Eight and One 64

Sergeant Crowell 101

James 139

Veronica Barclay

Hi, ho, Silver! Away! 39

Spot 74

No Fish Fridays 107

The Care and Feeding of Hobos 129

Loreen Barry

A Perfect Night 9

Four Small Poems 42

Silence 77

Haiku 128

Susan Bono

Flag Waving. 30

Eclipse 59

Something She Said 82

The Changing View 133

Myrna Fleckles

Three "Mykus" 17

Number 1 Bicycle. 57

Finality 98

Goals for Aging. 144

Vicki Frink

Whistle While You Work 19

The Shoe Gambit 63

Simple Pleasures 80

Ina Green

Living the Next Chapter 3

Through the Looking Glass. 56

One Day 78

Remaining in the Bud 143

Nancy Humphriss

Unforgettable 90th 10

Happy Anniversary. 52

The Pagoda 114

Nikki King

Happiness Defined 7

Apollo 62

Windows of Wisdom 137

Don Koss

A Mystery Solved 15

From Pulaski to Pā'ea 46

Twelve 87

Another Day, it's a Doctor Dey 121

Nancy Parsons

Reflections 5

The Princess and the Hair 70

The Plot 118

Hal Peters

Bad Bikinis 36

Carole Williams

Changing Norms 21

First Love 85

My Acting Debut. 111

Hildy Williams

A Soft Landing 1

The Big Fix 99

Geoff Withrington

The British Pub 44

Introduction

Until their work appears in print, writers are never sure which events, details, or themes will end up on the page. After composing, editing, revising, every tale is the sum of what's included and what's been left unsaid.

External circumstances also influence writers and their writing. The Varenna writers have carried on through fires and other natural disasters, a worldwide pandemic, social upheaval, and many personal tests. These events have left their marks on their stories, some obvious, others not. In recent years, the question, "What's next?" has made many feel uneasy.

But in this, our 12th year of publication, a sense of renewal has taken hold, with new people, new policies and programs here at Varenna. Our county's reservoirs are full after years of severe drought. There's always a lively crowd around the table at our meetings. We laugh a lot. "What's next?" is no longer a question so heavily colored by dread. There's still plenty of trouble in the world, but a spirit of rejuvenation infuses life at Varenna and is part of these stories, too.

Susan Bono, Editor

December, 2023

For those who make our stories worth telling

A Soft Landing
Hildy Williams

Two years ago, I took a leap and sold my home in order to help finance my move to Varenna. This was shortly after my husband passed away.

I walked away from the quaint wine country town of Healdsburg. Over a span of thirty-eight years I had built a strong community, raised a family, said goodbye to loved ones (parents, friends, husband), and chose change and something new for myself.

I admire people who take a really big leap and migrate far away from all that is familiar. I didn't become an ex-pat who settled in Mexico; I didn't even leave Sonoma County. In fact, I moved a little closer to my kids and grandchildren. One could say I made a lifestyle change but remained safely tethered to my support system and larger Sonoma County community. I've made new friends here at Varenna and I can see now how this small but vibrant community is getting familiar and comforting to me.

Still, the change has been pretty radical and quite difficult at times, about as different and challenging as I can personally embrace. This is the first time in my life I've lived alone. My apartment is all me. I've shed many of my pre-Varenna things, which just didn't work for me in my new digs.

Slowly, my family is beginning to understand and accept why I made this change. Perhaps they appreciate the fact that I am living in a very safe environment for a single lady in her later years. Perhaps they appreciate me not calling and asking for help with this and that around my house.

Going forward has been full of surprises. Far from being the least important aspect of life at Varenna is my special relationship with another resident. What an ideal place this is for a budding romance and friendship. Fine dining, cocktails, lovely walks and views. No Ubers or driving required.

Thank you, Varenna, for being my soft landing.

Living the Next Chapter
(In Retirement)
Ina Green

Those of us who live in a community where mostly everyone is retired wonder whether they are in a kind of school and living in a co-ed dorm. Just what kind of school is it? It isn't college or grad school!

However, we have come this far by passing courses in Childhood, Adolescence, Adulthood, and Middle Age. Many of us have even come through the gates of Old(er) Age. No one has failed, and we don't need grades or degrees to tell us who we are or what we have accomplished.

But this Univer-city offers continuing education in a subject called, "To Thine Own Self, Be True." There is no book for this subject. All one needs is a mirror. The course looks at experiences you've had and teaches you to trust yourself.

Another subject that is offered is called, "Love Thy Neighbor." Most people don't need this course. But because this is a community, we might need a refresher from time to time with remedial subjects in Flexibility, Patience, Empathy, Understanding, and Acceptance.

The price you pay for all this knowledge is Time.

Take advantage of the time you have been given and you will be granted a degree in Truth, Validation, and Friendship.

Turn your tassels to the other side—you have graduated!

Enjoy your next career!

Reflections
Nancy Parsons

Since we have been wearing masks for more than two years, I have not been wearing much makeup, especially lipstick. I mean, who cares, who even sees my lips? Now things are changing a bit and there seems to be much more facial exposure.

I was putting on my lipstick today, getting ready to come up to the Big House for writing class. I looked closely in the mirror and wondered, "Where did my upper lip go?" Is it another thing lost in aging or am I just examining myself more closely now that our new bathroom has a big mirror over the sink and nice bright lights in the ceiling?

Sometimes I look in the mirror and see my beloved aunt who lived to be 96. I smile and think, "Oh, how nice to see Aunt Mary Jane again." We always had a great time together and I never really thought of her as old.

Other times, especially after getting my hair cut short, I look in the mirror and see my sweet Uncle Marshall who was a pilot in the Air Force and always wore his hair very short. Once we visited the Officers Club and he treated me to my very first cocktail, a crème de menthe snow cone. He lived to be over 90 also.

I think of Aunt Lolly, who died just a few months short of 100. She was a real character, feisty, opinionated, and ramrod straight. She refused to use a walker because she did not want to get "stooped over." When I look at my hunched profile, I remember her and tell myself to "straighten up."

My parents died at age 59 and 61, so I have lived much longer than both of them. I often wonder what they would look like if they had aged as long as I.

This getting old business gives one so many opportunities to think of strange things, like upper lips or long-lived relatives. I'm trying to make peace with it.

Happiness Defined
Nikki King

Yesterday I caught myself out of the blue thinking, "I'm happy!" despite the fact that my shoulder was hurting, and my knee was painfully arthritic.

Why was I so happy?

Well, I had a lot of creative work to do and finally a place to display my work. I had joined a writing class and really enjoyed retrieving memories from my past and putting them on paper. I was getting my son Jordan's baby book together and organized.

In the years after my son's birth, I achieved some life goals that had eluded me throughout my hectic life in my younger years. I now felt great satisfaction about this. In addition to everything else, Varenna was offering a memoir class where our favorite pictures would be scanned and put into book form along with its matching picture pertaining to the memory. This was something I had always wanted but never had achieved.

Also, I had a renewed sense of gratitude and appreciation for my husband and his loving support. I was so happy to have his companionship.

I've been thinking about Leo Tolstoy's definition of happiness: "A quiet secluded life in the country, with the possibility of being useful to people to whom it is easy to do good, and who are not accustomed to have it done to them; then work which one hopes may be of some use; then rest, nature, books, music, love for one's neighbor—such is my idea of happiness."

I do feel it's important to help others and contribute in some small way to the betterment of the earth. But yesterday, all I thought of was my sense of well-being. Contentment to me equals appreciation and gratitude for what gifts I have been given.

This is my definition of happiness.

A Perfect Night
Loreen Barry

It is so very dark.

No streetlights or building lights, no home ablaze to spoil the velvet blackness.

We look up, to the sky. On the horizon, a new crescent moon.

And there, above us, the Milky Way.

Millions and millions of shining suns and galaxies, sending their light through time.

There is the Big Dipper, revealing the North Star, showing us the way.

The small reddish light, it must be Mars. The very bright "star," that's Venus.

Out of the darkness, an owl calls:

Who . . . who, who, who . . . who?

It's just us, here, looking through the darkness to the lights above . . . wondering.

Unforgettable 90th
Nancy Humphriss

As my January 27, 2023, birthday approached, I realized that I needed to warn my two sons and their wives that this momentous event was about to happen. I called them and told them that if they thought a bouquet of flowers with an "I love you, Mom" card was going, to make it, they needed to think again. I expected something special, and they ought to start planning.

Panic set in, as I expected, as together they tried to come up with ideas, such as a special dinner, a trip to San Francisco and a play, a night in Mendocino, etc. None of these fit the bill, so when I told them what I really wanted, they were both greatly relieved and enthusiastic. I announced that I wanted to go to a Sharks hockey game in San Jose. What 90-year-old woman would want to do this on her special birthday? I did!

When my sons were growing up in Rochester, New York, I introduced the whole family to this sport. The kids became talented players, and Dale and I, of course, took them to the practices and games, following their team through their teens. Moving to San Jose, hardly a hockey town then, they both found a high school team and played again. Since they were on the traveling team, one place we all loved to go was Santa Rosa where they played at the then-new rink made by Charles "Sparky" Schulz of *Peanuts* fame. He was often the referee. Because of all this, I, too, became a Sharks fan.

The plans were made, and on the Friday before the date, Andy and his wife, Vicki, drove from Reno to Santa Rosa and spent the night. In the morning, we drove to Kenwood, where Dale was now living in a memory care facility. His dementia wouldn't allow him to come with us, but we did stop to see him and took him out for his favorite meal, a McDonald's cheeseburger. It was during this weekend that we endured torrential rains, so we did a drive-through, which he loved, and we all enjoyed (or not) our cheeseburgers and fries.

After dropping him off, ready for a nap, we drove to San Jose. Eric, our son who lives in Pebble Beach, had made reservations at a classy Hilton Hotel where we each had a room. From the 15th floor I could look down at the city I had worked in for many years, but I recognized nothing, since it had become Silicon Valley personified. My large and beautiful room was decorated in gray, black, and white. There were three pictures on the walls, one in the bathroom, two in the bedroom, each one a photograph in black and white of computer keyboards. Hardly warm or pretty!

I had borrowed a wheelchair from Varenna. I knew I couldn't easily walk the distances down the long halls, and especially around the hockey rink, so my sons pushed me down the hall, into the elevator, and over to the cocktail lounge for some celebratory champagne. It was a great beginning to my birthday!

Eric had made a 5 o'clock reservation for dinner at a special downtown restaurant before the game started at 7:30. It continued to pour rain, but we managed to park close, since I had a handicapped placard. We entered the small but lovely restaurant and were met by the owner. He welcomed us to the bar, and when Eric told him we had reservations for 5:00, the owner said the dining room was closed! Not to be put off, Eric insisted he had made the reservation several weeks ago. So Pino, our host, checked his calendar, and announced, "Well I'll be damned! So you did! I decided to close tonight because the rain is so bad. I didn't think anyone would come. But the bar is open."

Eric told him he thought he should honor the reservation, especially because it was my 90th birthday. Both Pino and Eric were being friendly and eager to solve the problem. Whereupon Pino decided to invite us into the lovely but empty dining room, saying he loved to cook and would make anything on the menu we wanted, which he did. Andy had a rack of lamb, Vicki a steak, Eric something strange and exotic like a special Indian sushi, and I, not being very hungry, had crab fried rice and tasty green beans. Of course, wine was served as well. It took almost two hours to dine, and as we finished, Pino said he had made a special chocolate mousse in honor of my birthday. We had a wonderful time, both with family talk and delicious food. So special!!

We now had to hurry out in the pouring rain to get to the hockey game. Since I had a handicap placard, we were directed to a special entrance, which avoided the long, long regular line to get in. Once parked, I was pushed in my wheelchair to another special entrance where I was whisked up in an elevator to the top floor of the rink. We found our section where I stood while Andy pushed my wheelchair to a parking area and left it. We walked about twelve steps down to our seats with no problem.

Great seats and a most excited and happy feeling came over me. I actually had tears in my eyes from all the excitement, the noise, the lights, and the skaters below. And, of course, being with my family, everyone enjoying this special event!

I have to admit, we lost, but the Sharks did play a good game. At one point, Andy went up to buy some popcorn, and was surprised to find nothing could be paid for with a credit card, only cash. No matter what, even a big meal had to be in cash. Things have changed.

Back at our hotel, we all had a good night's sleep. The next morning, I was pushed down to the hotel restaurant where we all enjoyed a big breakfast. We said our goodbyes, and Eric headed back to Pebble Beach, while Andy, Vicki, and I returned to Varenna, stopping by for a short visit with Dale. That evening we had our dinner at Varenna, where I was yet again treated to champagne, some gifts, and birthday cake, along with the servers and other residents singing the appropriate song!

How perfect was my 90th! Even at 90, special memories can still be made.

A Mystery Solved
Don Koss

After twenty-two years, I'm closing my EarthLink account. They have been my email provider since somebody told me what email is. All in all, I would say that over the years there weren't that many problems.

However, when there was a problem, there was always too much hassle involved taking care of it. The cause of one of the hassles was finally answered today, when I decided to drop EarthLink and use the same email source that my wife is using: Comcast.

All interactions with EarthLink start with a security question. Mine is always, *"Your father's middle name?"* My father doesn't have a middle name. EarthLink always takes that as a wrong answer and goes through a time-consuming process to verify me in some other way. I have always asked them to change the question, so we don't have to go through this every time. They never would.

The last agent I talked to a couple weeks ago complicated the process even more. He hung up on me. I guess that was his idea of shortening the process.

When I called today, a woman with a heavy accent, Susan (really?), asks me the same question. I give her the story and the answer. She decides this is a problem for somebody else to deal with. She transfers me.

I get another agent, and, for the first time, I have an agent whose first language is English. He asks the same question. I tell him my father doesn't have a middle name and this is one of the problems I have with EarthLink. He verifies that my answer is correct and tells me they have the answer to that question as "None." Every other agent just thinks his middle name is "None." It doesn't get through to them (including the first woman I talked to today) that "None" means he doesn't have a middle name. According to all the agents at EarthLink, my father's name is Paul None Koss.

I'm not going to miss EarthLink.

Three "Mykus"
Myrna Fleckles

Author's note: As many of you know, Haiku is a very old form of poetry. It originated as part of Renga in Japan, and became Haiku, after Hokku in the late nineteenth century. The basic pattern for the three stanzas is five syllables, seven syllables, five syllables. In traditional haiku some parts of speech are not allowed. Poetic license has led me to "Mykus" with strict adherence to the 5, 7, 5 rule. The precision appeals to me, and the search for synonyms is both challenging and creative.

Popcorn

Popcorn, special treat!

Finally, shopped for crunchies.

Sweet and salty, yum!!

Oh, Baby

Baby boy at lunch,

So good, busy and happy.

So was his mother.

Changing Orbits

Earth still in orbit,
We in ours, changing daily.
Coping skills required.

Whistle While You Work
Vicki Frink

I have noticed that the word "chores" is only one letter different than the word "chorus" and have decided that this must be some otherworldly intervention, not just another of the English language's weirdities. Because I play music and often sing along whenever I find myself motivated to accomplish something worthwhile in my home, i.e., chores, to my admittedly twisted perception, "chores" and "chorus" are inextricably linked.

But—and this is important—not just any music is suitable for every chore.

For example, Bach is perfectly suited for ironing. The back and forth of the point and counterpoint reinforces the ironing motion so well that I might even want to take on one of my least favorite ironing tasks: tablecloths.

Vacuuming is best done to classic rock and roll, since you can easily dance with the vacuum cleaner, a stiff, but handy partner, preferably cordless.

Changing the sheets is much less tiresome when done to the lilt of Strauss waltzes, especially as you fling the top sheet in the air and sway.

And for some reason, bill paying is less stressful when singing along to Simon and Garfunkel.

One cautionary note: it is critical to avoid listening to Bach while driving, or you will find yourself sailing down the highway at 80 miles an hour and attracting unwelcome attention from the highway patrol. Note to self: They do not seem to be music lovers.

Changing Norms
Carole Williams

My parents, who focused much too much on things such as napkins in our laps and chewing with our mouths closed and putting our forks down between bites, would be very upset to see how little all that matters now. I took the approach with my kids that table manners allowed us to tolerate eating with other people, but I guess it doesn't apply to the families of today, who hardly ever eat together, anyway. Everyone is so busy and programed that most nights it's grab and run rather than the formal dinners my generation enjoyed. Or endured. I'm philosophical about this change, but I'm still trying to figure out how I feel about the relaxed rules of fashion.

What happened? When exactly did things change? It used to matter what we wore. I remember going to Forest Hills tennis tournaments in linen dresses and white gloves. I remember getting dressed up for the theater or a trip on an airplane. Now we see everything—boobs exposed, derrieres revealed, belly buttons with hardware, ripped clothing, gym clothes—everywhere. The motto now is "Anything goes" or "Wear whatever's most comfortable."

Maybe I'm too visual. I like seeing people dressed well. I like the respect for other people and institutions that taking the time to be thoughtful about dress implies. I like it, but I, too, have a closet full of suits and dresses I haven't worn in years because I'd be stared at and perhaps even laughed at in them.

Dressing up used to make us feel more sophisticated, more professional, and, no doubt, our behavior matched how we felt in those clothes. It's clear to me that behavior is often vastly improved if one is dressed well. Even today, schools that require uniforms report a decrease in rebellious behavior. At the extreme but now relevant end, uniforms don't allow kids to hide guns in their much-too-large pants. It's always been vital to "Dress for success" for a job interview. One strong opinion in favor of uniforms is that they enhance students' self-respect. Imagine that.

I wonder if there's a connection between the lax dress norms at USTA tournaments and the crowd feeling free to yell out whatever comes to mind, including slurs or chants or a loud, "Go Raffa!" just as he's starting to serve. Back when we wore dresses to Forest Hills, you could hear a pin drop until the audience politely clapped for good points. The whole audience respected the players' need to concentrate intensely. It was supposed to be a gentle sport back then. What happened?

I'm trying hard to care about the things that truly matter. It's a challenge adapting to so many changes as we age. The best we can do is choose when to maintain our own standards and try to keep silent about the rest. Lucky me; I can protest on paper!

Rugger
Bill Ardizoia

Baseball is a habit. The slowly rising crescendo of each game, the rhythm of the long season—these are the essentials and they are remarkably unchanged over nearly a century and a half. Of how many American institutions can that be said?
—Commentator George Will

Identity is defined as the characteristics determining who a person is. Most people identify themselves by an assortment of things: jobs, cars, clothes, houses, even shoes. My dad got his identity from baseball.

My dad was a good guy. He got along with almost everyone. He was proud of his Italian heritage, his family, and what he had accomplished. He was willing to say so to every person who would listen. He sailed over from Italy in 1921 as a young boy on the S.S. *Colombo* with his father and mother. He grew up, went to school, married, and volunteered to serve his adopted country in a world war. He built a life for his family from his professional career. There were no secrets: he worked hard, took responsibility, stayed out of trouble, and lived his dream as a pro athlete. He was loyal, maintained his friends, and had respect for everyone.

He played professional baseball for fifteen years and was one of only seven natives of Italy to play in the major leagues. He spent two spring trainings with the New York Yankees, one of which resulted in a two-inning stint against the old St. Louis Browns. He played in the Pacific Coast League for the Mission Reds, Hollywood Stars, Oakland Oaks, and Seattle Rainiers, and he finished his career with the Dallas Eagles of the Texas League.

He spent the bulk of his career in the PCL. Since transcontinental air travel had not developed to today's level, the PCL was unofficially considered to be a third major baseball league. Most of the travel in those days was by train and the usual team series was six or seven games as opposed to three these days.

In his 2021 book, *Lights, Camera, Fastball: How the Hollywood Stars Changed Baseball*, author Dan Taylor described him as follows: "[Rugger] Ardizoia was a chunky, hard-throwing San Franciscan, son of Italian immigrants. He signed with the Mission Reds [the day he graduated from high school] as a seventeen-year-old in 1937." The Reds were sold in 1938 to a Southern California group, who moved the team from San Francisco, and they became the Hollywood Stars.

In a 2005 interview for *This Great Game*, a website on baseball history, my dad was quoted as saying, "I loved playing in Hollywood. All the movie stars came to our games. In fact, I met Harry James, Ronald Reagan, the Marx Brothers, George Raft... Sinatra came out there... Rita Hayworth... I met them all... A lot of times I'd see Desi Arnez and Lucille Ball, and I'd sit down with them to shoot the breeze. I got along real good with all of them..."

He played with Hollywood in 1939 and 1940. In August 1940, the New York Yankees purchased his contract, and in the spring of 1941, he went to spring training for the first time with the big team but was sent down to the Kansas City Blues for more seasoning. World War II interrupted his career, though he continued to play on service teams as entertainment for the troops as a member of the Army Air Force. After the war, in 1946, he joined the Oakland Oaks, managed by Casey Stengel. In 1947, he again went to spring training with the Yankees. With those two innings he pitched for the Yankees against the Browns in 1947, it qualified him to be the oldest living Yankee before he died in 2015 at the age of 95.

He loved being with people, especially people who were interested in baseball. The stories were endless. He was acknowledged in Kostya Kennedy's 2011 book, *56: Joe DiMaggio and the Last Magic Number in Sports,* who wrote: "I enjoyed and was inspired by few conversations more than the several that I had talking baseball with Rugger Ardizoia and [his good friend, fellow San Franciscan, and former Yankee catcher] Charlie Silvera."

A local sportswriter who was familiar with our family name recently posed a question to me as to how he got his unusual first name: Rugger. My dad, whose given name was Rinaldo, grew up in the blue-collar neighborhood of Potrero Hill in San Francisco. On his way to school, he used to be chased by the neighborhood toughs and would jump into a thicket of star thistle, one of the most annoying plants on the planet. The bullies wouldn't chase him in there, tossing a comment over their shoulders as they ran off about him being a "rugged little bugger." Over time, the comment got shortened to "Rugger" and the name stuck.

He was a good cook and prepared meals for our family. He was particularly skilled at grilling and barbecuing. I think his skill came from having to learn how to cook in high school when his mother died. He had to have dinner ready for his father who worked as a laborer every day. I always thought he was a much better cook than my mother.

A lot of people remember my dad as a good pitcher. But Rugger was most proud of his ability with a bat, even though he only had one home run in his career. He was with Hollywood at the time, and he hit it against Seattle in 1947. My dad loved playing ball so much that I think he wished down deep to be known as a hitter so he could play every day instead of pitching every third or fourth day. I can remember going up to Balboa Park in our neighborhood in

San Francisco and he would have me shag balls for hours. Those hours running around the park were probably the reason I never took up baseball.

Most of the time, Rugger's personality was "live-and-let-live." But he did have a temper. He was slow to anger but could blow his top like an Italian volcano. That was something to behold!

One of my favorite pieces of memorabilia in his baseball collection was an old telegram from Clarence Rowland, then commissioner of the Pacific Coast League, dated August 2, 1948, and addressed to *Rinaldo Ardizoia, Ball Player, Hollywood Baseball Club.*

The way the Commissioner addresses him is significant. Those of you who have ever been in trouble with your teacher or parents know that when they call you by your given name—Rinaldo, in this case—they mean business and something unpleasant is about to happen. Mr. Rowland's telegram reads:

```
Rinaldo Ardizoia, Ball Player, Hollywood
Baseball Club.

Your actions make me think you wanted to
be put off the ball game. However for
filthy and vicious language used toward
Umpire Engle during the third inning of
the first game in Oakland Sunday August
1st and threatening to punch him in the
mouth you are fined twenty five dollars
which you will pay immediately or stand
suspended. Clarence Rowland
```

We can only imagine what was said between Rugger and the umpire. Twenty-five dollars may not seem like much, but players at the time were making far less than players today. I asked him one time about what he said and he just laughed. He promised to tell me some day. Never did.

There was another player and baseball philosopher of Italian descent named Berra. Not, as you might expect, Berra the Elder, known as Yogi, but Berra the Younger, his son, Dale Berra. Dale was a good ball player himself, playing in the major leagues for eleven years. He described Yogi in a way that was heartfelt and sincere. Dale said: "It's all about the way my dad carried himself all the time, with dignity, with respect for everyone. Not just opponents, but teachers and leaders. My dad respected all people, and he just happened to be a good ball player."

The same can be said about Rugger.

Flag Waving
Susan Bono

The 4th of July was less than a week away when I noticed my desire to fly a flag for the occasion. This seed was planted a few months earlier when I joined a gym that gives me a view of a car dealership's giant American flag whenever I'm on the treadmill. There's usually a stiff breeze from the west sending slow, luxurious ripples across Old Glory's enormous, striped face. I like the feeling I get when I watch those undulating waves, like I'm on a soft, slow-motion carnival ride. It connects me to times when I felt happy and safe. The older I get, the more comfort such associations give me.

We already had a flag somewhere in our garage—the one my parents flew from their front porch every July for decades. I had taken it when I sold their house 13 years ago, but we had never put it up.

"I didn't know you had any feelings about flags," my husband said when I mentioned my longing. "Let's do it."

"But we don't have a flag bracket," I said. "We never put the old one back up after we painted the house. You were worried about dry rot."

"We'll figure something out," he said. "I still have the bracket."

We have been married a long time, so I wasn't surprised when several days went by and nothing happened. But flags were on my mind when I met some friends at a hip coffee roastery in our small Bay Area town just north of San Francisco. I asked the group for their thoughts. They looked uncomfortable.

"Flags are creepy," one of them said.

"They've been co-opted by conservatives."

"But I love my flag," I said. "It belongs to me, too."

"Maybe if you flew it with something else, like a rainbow flag," someone suggested.

I replied, a little too loudly, that the Stars and Stripes represent everybody in America. Adding more colors doesn't fix anything. We quickly moved on to safer topics, but my heated response rattled everyone, including me.

As I left the café, I looked across the street and saw a flag hanging over the entrance to a car repair shop. I wanted to feel a surge of vindication. Here was some old-fashioned patriotism right in our progressive midst, but that flag made me uneasy. It was faded and wind-tattered after being left out in the weather too long. What might have started as a message about pride of country now looked like neglect and disrespect. Kind of creepy.

Driving home through one of our town's Victorian neighborhoods, I passed a few houses that sported flags or bunting. These decorations were dignified and handsome, their colors bright and strong. The sight of them calmed me and brought back fond memories of childhood summers. That was the effect I wanted. When I got home, I asked George to help me take our flag out of storage. It didn't take long to find it, but it took a while to get over my shock. This flag wasn't the one I'd imagined.

My parents loved the 4th of July and made an effort to celebrate it. They always served watermelon, corn on the cob, and homemade ice cream before the fireworks, and Mom decorated for the occasion, with everything from flag-inspired streamers to star-spangled cocktail napkins. In the pressure to empty their house and settle their affairs, I'd never really examined the one symbol of all those good times I had chosen to keep.

My parents' cotton flag hadn't been high quality to begin with, but now its white stripes were dull and stained. The fabric was gritty with dust, and there were even a few holes in it. I thought about displaying this sorry banner among my street's "Black Lives Matter" and "Follow the Science" lawn signs. What kind of message would that be sending?

While I pondered this question, I decided to wash the flag, carefully, by hand, the way I imagined my mother would have. I knew washing wouldn't take care of the stains or the holes, but as I worked, the fabric livened up in my hands. The soapy water turned deep brown, and I had to change the rinse water many times before it looked clear. But when I was finished, I knew my parents' flag would catch the wind more easily, and after ironing it, I thought it looked respectable. I carefully rolled it up and waited for my husband to find the bracket.

The flag was still in a corner of the kitchen on the 3rd of July. "If we're going to put up the flag this year," I said, "you need to install the bracket."

"I can't find it."

Somehow, I wasn't surprised.

"Can't we go buy another one?" I asked.

He looked shocked at the idea of buying something we already have. We both know how misplaced items turn up almost immediately whenever we do that. But we went to the hardware store anyway, and, after only a couple of reminders, on the afternoon of the 4th, he announced the job was done.

He hadn't asked me where I wanted the flag to go, and I didn't particularly like where he put it, but there it was, my parents' old flag, on a fencepost in the front yard, in lazy conversation with the summer breeze. I wasn't sure what message it was sending, but I didn't have time to worry, because I had to get ready for the neighborhood 4th of July party, which would put our flag to the test.

After making lemonade from our trusty Meyer lemons, I scrounged through my wardrobe, looking for something red, white, and blue. Nothing promising appeared. Why hadn't I kept any of my mother's holiday jewelry? I could picture her rhinestone flag pin. I had to settle for a red tee shirt and a blue neckerchief.

When I set my pitcher on the potluck table, I was pleased to see many of the younger women wearing flag-related apparel: flag earrings, red, white, and blue headbands, even jackets sporting stars and stripes. I wasn't sure if they were wearing these fashions ironically, but they seemed to enjoy the experience of displaying some patriotism.

One of my older neighbors greeted me. She keeps a low profile and avoids making political statements. It wasn't odd to see her wearing seafoam blue on Independence Day. But I was startled when she said, "I'm mad at my country right now. People who fly flags make me mad."

Was everyone thinking that way?

"Does that mean you're mad at me?" I asked.

"What are you talking about?"

"You just walked past our house. We've got a flag out!"

She laughed and I did, too. She hadn't noticed, and maybe nobody else had, either. And why would it matter on this street where everyone was just trying to be friendly and have a good time? With all the kids darting around and the aroma of barbeque smoke mixing with the sound of laughter, I felt like I was far away from any place where my choice of outdoor decorations would be in any way dangerous.

"That's what so great about living in this country," I said. "You can be mad at it and say so."

"I can't argue with that," my neighbor replied. "At least not in theory."

I grabbed a plate and moved closer to the barbeque, glad that my flag was somehow part of this community we'd created, one that held up, even during the Pandemic. I glanced over at a "Follow the Science" placard on another neighbor's lawn. It was crooked on its stakes and faded after almost three years outside. It had been a long time since I'd really looked at any of those signs. I wondered if anybody else had, either.

Bad Bikinis
Hal Peters

Author's Note: *Since these stories are quite personal, I got my wife's permission to relate them.*

In the early 1960s, the bikini was making its initial appearance in the U.S. Its popularity in Europe was already established. Starting in 1962, I had a sales representative's position with Jantzen Sportswear. I sold their men's and women's golf attire, but I could personally purchase any of their merchandise, which included swimwear.

Before leaving our Southern California home for a brief July vacation to visit my mother in Marin County, I bought my wife, Renee, her first bikini. During our stay, we decided to take a respite from the heat in Mom's pool. Seated poolside were three elderly couples, Mom's friends from church, who had been invited to lunch.

Renee was putting our young son down for a nap while I was enjoying the water, so she appeared after me. All eyes were on her as she exited the house and walked to the edge of the pool. Her striking "Miss Marin County 1956" figure enhanced her recently manufactured powder-blue bikini. She entered the water and gracefully swam to my end of the pool, where the three men and their spouses were seated. As she began to lift herself out near where I was perched on the diving board, I thought, "Oh, my God!" and as discreetly as possible said, "Get back in the water, I'll get you a towel and meet you at the other end of the pool."

My reason for concern: the suit was totally transparent! Had she emerged in front of the guests, "embarrassed" would have been an understatement.

Later that afternoon, I notified the Portland, Oregon, factory of the problem. They were extremely grateful and pulled it from their Holiday line.

Four years later, I had changed employers and was selling golf clothing for Catalina Sportswear, a Southern California manufacturer who also made swimwear. The Christmas holidays were a perfect time for a sales rep's vacation, as retailers had their merchandise and didn't need to see salesmen. Renee and I joined another couple in Acapulco for a ten-day getaway.

We'd learned to be prepared. I purchased three bikinis from the newest models not yet in the stores. We enjoyed swimming, water-skiing, deep-sea fishing, and sightseeing for several days before Bad Bikini Number Two appeared.

Renee had picked out a purple floral bikini to wear that day. It was a beautiful suit that fit perfectly. It was her favorite and it was easy to see why. As she was drying off after her "before dinner" shower, I said, "Renee, get a load of yourself in the dresser mirror." She gave me a puzzled look until she saw herself.

"Oh, my God!" she gasped.

Everywhere the suit had been, her skin had absorbed its purple dye! It seemed Renee was an unknowing guinea pig for a second manufacturer.

We simultaneously exclaimed, "How do we get this off?" We scrubbed with soap and a washcloth for a long time before we got rid of the purple. Catalina was notified to cancel production of that model, and, like Jantzen, was grateful for the information and replaced the defective swimwear on our return. Shortly after this incident I left Catalina, and future swimwear was bought in retail stores.

No more problems.

Hi ho, Silver! Away!
Veronica Barclay

I absolutely HATE sweeping the floor—any floor—any time—for any reason! I began developing this hatred as a young child whenever my mother found I had "borrowed" the kitchen broom to convert it into my homemade hobby horse. Since my parents would not buy me a horse or pony, my sturdy steed was crafted from whatever materials I could salvage from our garage and yard.

It would only take me about twenty minutes to transform the once-naked broomstick into a magnificent parade equine or sturdy trail horse, ready to explore my backyard and neighborhood. Using several white mop strings liberated from the wet mop stabled right next to the kitchen broom "stall," I carefully cut and stapled a flowing mane and tail along one side of the painted gray broom handle. Occasionally, I would adorn him with a leather bridle made from the rawhide boot laces found in my dad's high-top work boots. Once, I found a bright red cardinal feather on the ground and saved it for the 4th of July, when I pretended we were the Grand Marshal in the annual holiday parade.

I named my trusty steed Silver, after the famous TV horses ridden by the Lone Ranger. Together, we would gallop through the halls and bedrooms, jump over cardboard boxes and tools, pretending they were bridges and cacti scattered throughout our imaginary desert or mountain trails.

Together we were invincible, fighting imaginary wrongs, and searching for buried gold or bankrolls I promised to give to the poor, if I ever found any. We were a polite duo, too—always stopping to chat with any neighborhood cat we encountered on our path, offering a quick pet and rub behind their ears. After performing my good deeds, I would gather my reins, raise my arm, and yell, "Hi ho, Silver! Away!"

And then it would happen. From out of nowhere, my mother would suddenly appear before me, demanding that I clean up her broomstick and sweep the kitchen floor. Busted before my playtime was over, I had to cut my horseback riding short and deconstruct Silver's parade-worthy mane and tail, careful not to miss one strand of his flowing mane or a single finger-ripping staple. After throwing away the evidence in the outdoor garbage can, I slowly returned my steed to the kitchen.

My mom would be waiting there for me, both hands perched on her hips for emphasis, ready to bark specific orders on how I needed to make sure I got every single cracker crumb or dead insect that may have been wedged in between a table or chair leg. No matter how hard I tried to please her, it was never satisfactory.

I usually ended those sweeping sessions totally exasperated, with my mom sucking her teeth and declaring, "THIS is how you sweep and clean a kitchen floor!" Then she would personally demonstrate how to put your whole weight behind each stroke of the broom, as if a breadcrumb might try to run and hide in some crack between cabinets. It was maddening, and I could not hide my disgust, with my arms crossed or eyes scanning the ceiling. The worst part always came at the end, when she pounded the broom bristles on the slick floor and caught my barefoot toes in my flip flops. How irritating!

And that's when I learned how to twirl in a perfect U-turn and lope away—horseless—yelling, "Hi ho, Silver! Away!"

Four Small Poems
Loreen Barry

Tao

Creation in Silent Space

Seed of the Tao

Sprouts in Silent Light

We

From the Earth

On the Earth

Back to the Earth

Bequeathed to us

Bequeathed

Even now
The Immortal One glides
Even now he glides
Even now

The stones at the bottom
Appear to be moving
Clear running water

The Joys of the British Pub
Geoff Withrington

There's something I wish I didn't love so much: the British pub! I have lived in many countries around the world—and visited many more. What is the one thing I really miss when I am away from my own country, England? It is the British pub.

The pub is a unique institution, and I have never found its equal anywhere else in the world. Sure, there are bars in almost every country, but none of them have the atmosphere and camaraderie of the British pub.

During the ten years we lived in a hamlet on the south downs of England, our local hostelry was the George & Dragon. If ever I wasn't home on time, Shirley knew exactly where I was: in the pub! She would sometimes call the George & Dragon and ask the publican—my old mate, Howard McNamar—if I was there.

Howard would say, "Just a moment, Shirley, let me see." He would then cover the mouthpiece and shout to me, "Geoff, it's Shirley, are you here?"

I would usually say, "I'm on my way!" and leave to walk down the lane to our home. Sometimes I would say,

"No!", and he would say, "No, Shirley, he's not here. I'll send him home if he comes in."

I remember on one occasion I said "No," but Shirley was wise to that. Five minutes later, she burst through the door carrying our two very young sons in her arms. "Geoff!" she shouted across the bar, "These are your children. Would you like to meet them?"

I learned a lesson and was never so late again. I don't even need a place to escape, but boy, how I miss the pub!

From Pulaski to Pā'ea
Another *It Was a Dark and Stormy Night Adventure*
Don Koss

It was a dark and stormy night. It's the small town of Pulaski in the southeast corner of Iowa. The town of 263 people is struggling through one of the worst storms of the last decade. It looks like the annual Pulaski Corn Show Parade might be called off.

Carlton Osgood doesn't really care. He's in Pā'ea in the suburbs of Pape'ete on the island of Tahiti. The temperature is 78° and it rained for about half an hour this afternoon. He's never even heard of Pulaski, although he does like corn. And he does like parades. A corn parade might be fun.

(Why does our story start in Pulaski? That's a story for another book. This story does start in Pulaski. It may end in Pulaski. I don't know. I haven't gotten that far yet.)

(Now I have.)

Janie June Watkins is a young girl in her early twenties who has lived in Pulaski all her life. It was sometime during her schooling that she discovered there were other cities beyond Pulaski, and now she's wondering if maybe there is a way to see one of those cities.

As luck would have it, she had entered the Corn Club of Iowa Wordle Competition and forgotten all about it.

Now she gets a call from the president of the Corn Club, Osgood Morton, telling her she has won second prize and has a choice of a year's supply of lime Jell-O or all the corn she can eat in one day or an all-expense trip to a city she can hit with a dart on a map with her eyes covered.

Again, as luck would have it, somebody switched maps. She throws the dart, and can you believe it? She hits Pā'ea. The organizers are still trying to find out what happened to the map of Iowa. Some practical joker cost the Corn Club the next three years of their budget when they replaced the map of Iowa with a map of Tahiti.

Janie June's first challenge is to get from Pulaski to Pā'ea. There are no flights out of Pulaski. The closest airport is in Bloomfield, about ten miles to the west, but she has to go another 53 miles to Kirkland to get a flight to anywhere. And there are no direct flights to Pā'ea. She will have to get to Cedar Rapids. That's a two-hour drive, and public transit seems to be a problem out of Pulaski. She talks to Wally who owns Wally's Taxi Service.

Wally started his taxi service when he was sixteen. He used to drive his grandmother from the General Store to the Pulaski Mennonite Church. He thought that if he could manage that five-minute, three-and-a-half-mile trip without getting lost, maybe he could make some money carrying passengers.

He was wrong.

Wally still doesn't go any farther than eight miles from the General Store.

It's about a thirty-seven-hour walk to Cedar Rapids, so that may not work out either.

Finally, the problem is solved. The town social club, The Women of Corn, holds a bake sale and raises the money to hire an Uber to make the run to Cedar Rapids. What a stroke of luck. They find an Uber driver who really likes corn.

(I'm skipping the part where she has to get all the paperwork required to enter French Polynesia. This is supposed to be a short story.)

Traveling with her backpack given to her by her Girl Scout Troop, she's on her way. She will fly from Cedar Rapids to Chicago to San Francisco to Pape'ete on the island of Tahiti. A pleasant 17 hours and 23 minutes of bonding with flight attendants who weren't thinking of 17-hour-and-23-minute flights when they applied for this job. In Pape'ete she will then have to find a taxi to take her to Pension Te

Miti where she has a room for $59 a night. She's hoping the Corn Club is paying for more than one night.

Meanwhile, in Pā'ea, Carlton Osgood is thinking it's about time he moves on from Tahiti. He plans on going to the airport and getting on the first plane that has an open seat.

(I don't think you can do that. Passports, visas, and other requirements. Maybe he's thinking of only local flights.)

(No, it's a United Airlines flight to San Francisco. I'm going to go with that. Maybe nobody will notice.)

Could there be something to the fact that his name is Carlton Osgood and the President of the Corn Club is Osgood Morton?

It's San Francisco International Airport, SFO. Two planes are landing within minutes of each other. One from Pape'ete, French Polynesia, and one from Chicago, Illinois. Passengers with connecting flights walk to various gates and waiting areas. Carlton Osgood clears customs and heads for United's Global Lounge to see if he can catch another flight and to see where he will be travelling.

A young girl gets off the flight from Chicago and is told her connecting flight is delayed, and because this story is pure fantasy, she is given access to United's Global Lounge. The young girl and the gentleman from Tahiti arrive at the Global Lounge at nearly the same time. They walk through the Lounge to the dining area. There is an agent at the entrance. He greets the young lady, then turns to Osgood and greets him.

"There will be a short wait," he tells both of them.

"There's nobody in the room," says Osgood.

The young lady stands quietly. Pretty much in awe of the whole situation.

The host turns to both and announces, "I have two tables available."

He seats them at the two available tables and walks into the kitchen. In minutes, he returns. He is no longer wearing his jacket. He has menus in his hand. He takes their orders and announces that nothing on the menu is available. All he can serve is the assorted cheese plate and today's assortment is Swiss.

"Try not to break the toothpick. We don't have many left."

"Where's the rest of your staff?" asks Osgood.

"United is cutting back a little. It's the slow season, you know."

Osgood finishes his meal, both pieces of cheese, gets up, and leaves the room.

The young lady finishes one piece and asks for a takeout box for the other one. She leaves the room.

They both barely notice another young lady waiting at the entrance. It's Janie June Watkins of Pulaski, Iowa.

That night it stormed in Pulaski, Iowa. It was 78° in Pā'ea.

Happy Anniversary
Nancy Humphriss

Our third anniversary was approaching, and Dale said he was planning something special. We were living in Belleville, Indiana, where Dale was flying jets with the Air Force, and I was being a wife and mother. We had an eight-month-old daughter, so I was really looking forward to a time alone with my husband. My thoughts centered on a trip for a special dinner across the Mississippi River, which separated us from St. Louis, or maybe even an afternoon seeing "Oklahoma" at an outdoor theater known for its wonderful musicals. Dale said he'd already talked to our friends who were willing to watch our daughter.

On the day of our anniversary, Dale got me in the car and drove away from the city for several miles out in the countryside. I was confused, but ready to see what was going to happen. We drove to what seemed to be a small airport with several small planes parked near what appeared to be the runway. It was not paved, just short grass and dirt. On one of the planes was a big sign saying, "Happy Anniversary Nancy!"

I was both surprised and somewhat uncertain about what was about to happen. Dale was so excited and told me since I had never been in an airplane, he wanted to treat me to my first ride. He had gotten his commercial license, so he could now take civilian passengers up. "You're going to love it," he said. "It's so beautiful to look down on the earth below and zip through the clouds and blue sky."

I wasn't sure I was ready for this, but yes, it might be exciting and fun. He got me in the plane, a two-seater, the pilot in front, the passenger behind. He seatbelted me and got in the seat ahead of me where the controls were. He started the engine, propellers whirling, and we slowly moved over the bumpy, grassy runway. As we went faster and faster, suddenly the wheels left the ground, and we soared up over the trees.

I was immediately overcome with panic and fear and started hitting Dale on the back of his head, telling him I didn't like this and wanted to get back down immediately. He tried to assure me all was well, and I should relax and enjoy it. He said, "Look, Nancy, down below we are flying over the Mississippi. See how big and blue it is!"

By now I was actually crying with my eyes closed and begging Dale to go back. I had my arms around his neck, and he shouted to me to let go; he couldn't handle the controls with my hands around his neck. When he finally realized I was not able to control my fear, he circled around, preparing to land. After the plane landed and we got out and on the ground again, he just held me until I settled down. He apologized, telling me he had no idea I was so afraid of heights. In the car on the drive home, we just sat and were silent.

Although he didn't mention this, I realized he had spent a lot of money to rent the plane which, of course, he wouldn't get back. After I apologized, he went to pick up our daughter, and we had a quiet lunch. He decided to go back to work, and I took a relaxing nap. This was the end of our anniversary.

In the days that followed, our friends, most of them pilots and their wives, made me feel I was in disgrace. The couples often went to interesting places in the private planes they rented, enjoying both the flying and the places they could visit, which were too far to drive to. I felt guilty making Dale miss all the fun, but no way was I going to get on the plane again!

Several months later, due to a family crisis, circumstances made it necessary to fly commercially. I dreaded this, but I knew I had to face up to my responsibility. Dale didn't go with me, since he could fly for free in an Air Force plane, so I took our daughter with me.

Once seated, the plane seemed so much safer, with sturdy metal wings, lots of people, and bigger all over. Once we got in the air, I was nervous, but I managed to relax a bit. From then on, we did fly often for travel, and while I never enjoyed it, I knew it was the only way to go.

My fear of heights stays with me still. Many times, when driving through lovely mountains, like, for instance, in Norway, when others in the car are exclaiming at the beauty of the sheer cliffs the road is taking us over, I am on the floor of the car in the back seat, covering both my eyes and my ears, not able to enjoy the wonderful sights they are seeing. Some inner fear was established years ago, and I must live with it.

Through the Looking Glass
Ina Green

Five-foot-two and blonde

Became four-foot-eleven and bland

Stick your nose in the air

Or your head in the sand

No repair or demand

Can change what the mirror reflects

So don't expect

That the past will be present

Or that you can't resent

(Of course you can resent)

Whatever change

Has rearranged that reflection in the mirror

Number One Bicycle
Myrna Fleckles

When I was seven, my parents gave me a shiny, blue, balloon-tire bicycle as a summer surprise. I was over the moon. Our neighbor, Fern Huntsinger, who lived across the street, offered her eight-year-old son, Bobby, to teach me to ride it. So, my probably very relieved father happily left for his office.

Bobby and I admired the bike while he prepared to send me down the smooth sidewalk. As he held the bike steady, I sat, wobblily, on the seat. He showed me how to grip the handlebars and where to put my feet, then gave the rear wheel a slap and said, "Get going."

Well, I did, but quickly fell sideways into a soft bed of non-prickly succulents. He righted me. I got up, unscathed and determined to try again. That time, I actually pedaled and moved farther before landing on the edge of a neighbor's lawn with no harm done to me nor the blue beast that threw me. We continued trying until I reached the end of the block, stopped in triumph, upright, on my own, and decided to wheel the, by then, friendlier bike back to my own yard, where our mothers heard our tale and offered milk and cookies.

From then on, Bobby and I rode often, exploring our neighborhood and beyond. He proved to be a good friend, and I continued bike riding long into adulthood and marriage, never forgetting my adventures on the beautiful, blue, balloon-tire surprise!

Eclipse
Susan Bono

B ack in those faraway days, my parents were always showing us kids something. When our family drove the winding levee roads along the Sacramento River in winter, my mother pointed to rounded clumps of dark vegetation caught in the branches of bare trees. "Look! Mistletoe!" she would sing out, time after time, as if each sighting was a small miracle. "And that's a hop dryer," she might tell us as we rounded another bend and looked down into the farms and fields protected from the river.

It didn't matter that my little brother and I had only the vaguest notion of what hops or mistletoe were. My parents believed in building our understanding like a mosaic, each little chip of information becoming part of a larger picture. Sometimes it was like being inside a kaleidoscope, the kind with shards of colored glass that glowed when you aimed the end you twisted toward the sunlight. Whenever I discovered an especially beautiful pattern, I always wanted to keep it. But even then, I knew that life is full of tiny pieces that are forever shifting.

One morning when I was about five, my father called a bunch of neighborhood kids into our backyard. My mother was looking after my brother, which meant I was being treated like one of the big kids. Dad had fixed up a cardboard box he got at the Purity Market with a pinhole on one end and a piece of white paper taped inside on the other.

"This is for watching the eclipse," he told us. "Here, Susan, you try it."

I didn't know what an eclipse was, something to do with the sun, which we weren't supposed to look at. But today my dad was telling me to stand with my back to the sun and put a box on my head so it would be safe to see it.

I'd always been nervous in crowds, and now I was being singled out in front of Jimmy and JoAnn Allen, Susie Wilson, Rudy Tibbs, and Tommy Hickman to suffer what felt like some strange humiliation. I didn't know how to protest. My parents were always showing us things, and most of the time it was something we never expected, like magnets attracting and repelling, or balls of silver thermometer mercury dividing at the touch of a pin. Just because I had a bad feeling about this one, like maybe an eclipse was something scary, I couldn't refuse the opportunity to learn something.

So, there I was with a box on my head, breathing smells of paper pulp and glue, the world around me hidden, listening to the other kids shuffling in the grass around me.

"Do you see it?" my father asked eagerly, but I didn't know what I was supposed to be looking at. It felt like a trick designed to make me feel stupid. I burst into tears, but I didn't want to pull my head out of the box because the big kids would see me crying. After a little tug of war with my dad, I was liberated from the box, but not from my embarrassment. I ran off for a while to collect myself.

When I cautiously returned to the group, everyone ignored me. They were too busy listening to my dad and waiting for their turn. As I watched them gamely following instructions, looking for the magic my father claimed was in that box, I could imagine it then, the eclipse. I could see it somehow. As if through a pinhole of my own thoughts.

Apollo
Nikki King

I want to tell you about a 2,000-year-old redwood tree that continues to live and thrive in my neighbor's yard near my Russian River cabin. As I drive that small road to my cabin, I look forward to seeing my massive old redwood friend whom I have named Apollo. This ancient old redwood has split in two and grows straight up into the sky 250 feet high! The leaves are dark green, narrow, flat, and arranged in two alternating ranks. This ancient redwood is unlike any other you've ever seen because of its location. It lives alongside the road in a small lot, obscuring the cabin at the end of the yard.

Redwoods grow *only* in California!

In the early 19th century, redwoods were found all over the area. Back then, loggers came into this location and removed all the redwoods until only one tree remained. My redwood, Apollo! It survived because it was often underwater and difficult to cut down. What luck!

How fortunate we are to enjoy this magnificent tree near our cabin.

The Shoe Gambit
Vicki Frink

My husband doesn't understand why I have so many pairs of shoes, and, I must admit, he may be justified. I love shoes, and I especially love shoes with unusual colors or patterns. As a result, I often end up with single-use shoes—that is, shoes I can only wear with one outfit. But I have cleverly handled this issue by buying additional outfits just to match the unusual shoes. In the life game of clothing challenges, it is game, set, and, especially, matched. My husband just shakes his head.

Ohhh . . . Eight and One
Bill Ardizoia

If lessons are learned in defeat, our team is getting a great education.
—Former University of Minnesota Football Coach Murray Warmath

In my senior year of high school, I was elected co-captain of the Archbishop Riordan football team. Riordan, at the time an all-boys high school of around 700, was in the southern part of San Francisco. We were generally from working-class families living in row houses in the outer Mission district and from Daly City. Riordan opened in 1949, new compared to the other Catholic high schools in the city—Sacred Heart and St. Ignatius—both dating back to the 1800s. We were a member of the tough Catholic Athletic League with Bellarmine, Serra, and St. Francis from the Peninsula and St. Mary's, Bishop O'Dowd, and St. Elizabeth's from the East Bay. Sacred Heart and St. Ignatius played in the City League.

We played our games on Friday nights at Kezar Stadium, the home of the 49ers of the NFL. Kezar was built in the 1920s and was unique in more ways than one. It was a thrill for opposing teams to play there on Fridays, and on

Sundays, they could see the same stadium filled with raucous fans cheering for the Niners on TV.

The unique qualities of the stadium are colorfully described in David Talbot's 2012 book, *Season of the Witch: Enchantment, Terror, and Deliverance in the City of Love:*

> Until 1971, the 49ers played in the heart of the city in rough and rowdy Kezar Stadium, a neighborhood arena squeezed between Golden Gate Park and the Haight. Going to games at Kezar was not for the faint of heart. [Following the game] as the Niners fled the field into the dark, dirt-floored tunnel that led to their locker rooms, they were often bombarded with beer and whiskey—*some of it still in cans and bottles.* Wise players kept their helmets on as they headed toward the tunnel of doom.
>
> Screeching seagulls swooped overhead splattering fans below with their foul white glop. Over the years, the benches [in the spectator stands] became so saturated with seagull dropping that you couldn't help but take the stench home with you on the seat of your pants . . . Brawls were a common occurrence, making the stands more dangerous than the field.

Our experience on Friday nights was different. We drew about 1,500 fans, mostly students and families and friends of the players, including those from the opposing team, in a stadium that seated 60,000. The few fans made the old stadium even more dark and gloomy. It was usually chilly, and the damp fog blew in through the park from the ocean. You could see the wisps through the lights that barely illuminated the playing field, which added to the dreariness.

I will never forget the smell of the field. It was a mixture of damp soil, the slightly fishy odor from the seagull offerings, and the faint scent of sweat, spit, and who-knows-what-else from prior games. The middle of the field was worn out from all the other contests and was mostly sand, which the groundskeepers threw down to accompany the few brave tufts of grass. Plays up the middle were like running on the beach.

Our coach, when asked about our prospects for the season for one of the local papers, stated that our team was going to be Riordan's "best ever." Well, it didn't quite turn out that way. Because of a combination of injuries, tough competition, and bad luck, we didn't notch a win in our first eight games. We only had one more to go to try to salvage our miserable season.

The final game, my last game at Kezar, was against St. Mary's of Berkeley. The Panthers took the field with sharp white jerseys and red pants. They also were one the last teams to wear those brown MacGregor leather helmets with the cross on the top. (The Golden Boy, Paul Hornung, wore one when he was at Notre Dame. They looked like you could fold them up and put them in your back pocket after the game.) We were in our usual purple jerseys with gold helmets and pants, and high purple socks like the pros wore. I think the high socks were an attempt to keep our legs warm in the foggy chill.

We were evenly matched; St. Mary's had only won two games that season. As would be expected, from the opening kickoff, neither team could establish any sort of momentum. It was 0-0 at halftime. The game continued to be tight into the fourth quarter, a defensive struggle in the sandpit in the middle of the field.

With five minutes left on the clock, St. Mary's intercepted a pass and ran it back for a touchdown, but missed the extra point. We all thought that this might be an opening to win the game if we could score a touchdown in the remaining time, plus successfully kick an extra point.

Sure enough, with only a couple of minutes left in the game, we recovered a fumble on St. Mary's ten-yard line. A win might still be in the cards!

It was third down, and we called a sweep right with an alley-oop pass to the right corner of the end zone to our wingback, Curtis Green. Curtis really couldn't see all that well and wore these black plastic horned-rim glasses under his helmet. It was an odd sight—kind of like an owl with shoulder pads and a helmet on his head.

Tailback Joe Sobeck, a good athlete who later played at Nevada-Reno, took the snap, sprinted right, and floated the ball to Curtis, who was wide open in the end zone. As the ball arced downwards, Curtis must have lost the ball in the glare from the lights. Or his glasses fogged up. Maybe he was distracted by a swooping seagull. As he tried to catch the ball, it slipped through his arms like it was greased. There was a loud, "Oooohhh!" as the crowd groaned in disappointment. So did our team.

When Curtis came back to the huddle, he was distraught, his eyes filled with tears and pleading, "Run it again, *please*, run it again."

Now by this time, St. Mary's was wise to what happened, and thought that we might try it again. You could see their defense shading over to our right to guard against it. Our coach sent in another play. But Sobeck looked at Curtis, still crying and pleading for another chance, then at me as one of the captains. So did everyone else in the huddle.

Joe said, "What do you think?" I looked around the huddle at the other players, their breath like steam in the foggy cold. I looked at Curtis, who was a good friend. I knew he was hurting, embarrassed, and wanting another chance.

I didn't think too hard about it. I swallowed, looked around, and said, "Run it again." Curtis ran out to his position...*and took off his black horned-rim owl glasses and flung them to the sideline!*

Sobeck sprinted to the right once again. He evaded a fierce rush, as St. Mary's had correctly anticipated the play.

Joe lobbed the ball over their arms in the direction of Curtis in the corner of the end zone.

It then turned surreal and was like in the movies where it goes quiet and everything is in slow motion. But the focus turns way up and that is the way it really happens!

Curtis was surrounded by two or three St. Mary's guys. They were all over him, but Curtis outjumped them and made an unbelievable catch. We all mobbed him with joy because we had tied the game.

Of course, in all the excitement, our team got disorganized, and we were penalized five yards for delay of game. The extra five yards was a little too much for our feeble kicker, and he shanked the extra point. The game ended in a 6-6 tie—the only blemish on an otherwise winless season.

I sometimes think of Curtis, without his owl glasses, getting a second chance, trying as hard as he could, and making that unbelievable catch in the mist and fog at smelly old Kezar. To this day, I don't know if Curtis ever retrieved his glasses from the sidelines.

After that season, people would ask our coaches and our players how the year went for Riordan's football team. Without exception, we would always say, "Ohhh, [pause] eight and one. Pretty good, huh?"

The Princess and the Hair
Nancy Parsons

Once upon a time, in a land far away, there lived a shy little princess who had big hair issues, although at this time so long ago, these hair issues did not have a name. The princess's mother, Mrs. Queen, a petite, pretty, natural blonde, was constantly fretting over her daughter's hair, which she called "mouse brown" and "as straight as sticks." Every morning, from the time the little princess had enough hair to hold together, Mrs. Queen would tightly braid the mouse brown hair to keep it from getting in the little princess's eyes and thereby causing, in Mrs. Queen's words, her "eyes to cross."

Of course, Mrs. Queen's hair was always perfectly coiffed, having been washed and finger-waved every Friday afternoon at Leota's Beauty Parlor, which was down on the corner of 4th and Race Street, just beyond the post office, but not quite as far as the creek.

One day when the little princess was about four years old, and her only brother, the little prince, was just over two, Mrs. Queen decided to have the children's portrait taken at the photography department of JCPenney's department store.

In preparation for the portrait day, Mrs. Queen went into second gear! She made sure the little boy's bright yellow romper suit was laundered and pressed, his little white high-top shoes were polished, and his beautiful thick hair was cut to perfection by Frankie, the barber.

Because of the hair issues, preparations for the little princess took much longer. About two weeks before the photo event, Mrs. Queen took the little princess to Leota's Beauty Salon to have her very first permanent wave.

Leota's Salon was in the big front room and dining room of her home on Fourth Street. It was a magical place, full of lights, mirrors, make-up, pleasant perfume, magic wands, movie magazines, and the sounds of women chattering and exchanging gossip.

Or, depending on how you viewed the room, it could also be said that it was a scary place, rather like a torture chamber, full of loud, shiny helmets, magic potions, and stinky smells. Long, low sinks lined a wall, and adjacent to the sinks were hoses that squirted water. Combs, brushes, jars of bobby pins, little metal curlers, plus bottles and jars full of unknown liquids covered the counter tops. Big red leather chairs sat under the huge shiny helmets which noisily spewed out hot air on the ladies' heads.

With great trepidation, the little princess did as she was told and climbed up on a big chair that was backed up close to the sink. Leota covered her body with a heavy brown rubber cape, told her to scooch down in the chair, and *voila*, the back of the chair fell down, and her head was in the wash bowl being sprayed by very cold water.

From this point, and for about an hour, the little princess has no memory of what happened to her and her hair. But, to continue, after an hour or so, she climbed up on another chair.

At this time, the little princess had big heavy metal rollers in her thin mousy brown hair. Leota attached the rollers to magnetic clips that were connected to long wires, which were then attached to a contraption that looked rather like a chandelier or something that might be found in a prison, used for an execution. Leota then turned on the heat, and, with the flick of a switch, in about ten minutes, the little princess became a little girl with brown mousy curly-kinky hair worthy of a memorable portrait from JCPenney's.

Mrs. Queen was delighted with the change in her daughter's hair. The little princess was not totally sure about the entire procedure. It was too long to sit, too many bad smells, just plain too boring. However, it did have a few perks. There were *Photoplay* magazines with lots of pictures of movie stars! And the big chair that was under the hot chandelier was situated right by a window that looked into Leota's back yard.

Leota happened to be married to a real live prince who worked in the circus as a wild animal trainer. Prince Kiyagore traveled all over the country with his tigers, but on this particular day of the little princess's inauguration into permanent waves, the real prince was on holiday and spending time with Leota. His tigers, who had accompanied him, were eating their lunch while lounging in their cage in Leota's backyard, which was directly under the little princess's window where she sat to have her first perm.

It turned out to be the most memorable day with curls!

Epilogue

One day, in the not too long ago, when the little princess had grown up and was working on "all her issues," she entered her lovely powder room and faced herself in her lighted mirror. Her mouse brown hair was thinning, turning gray, and ready for yet another permanent. All of a sudden, the old princess thought, "I've had enough curls in my life, I'm going to embrace my straight hair." And so, after having four perms a year for sixty years, for a grand total of 240 perms, the little old princess with straight gray hair stopped cold turkey! And she lived happily ever after.

Spot
Veronica Barclay

Spot was the name of the tiny brown and white porcelain dog that lived at the end of the row of salt and pepper shakers near the stove in my grandma's kitchen. He was chocolate brown, except for one little white spot on his left side.

Made of fragile bone china, he was nestled in a fancy gold earring box from Milens Jewelers in downtown Oakland. The tiny box was wedged between a bud vase and the Sunday cloth napkins, protected from Grandpa's extra-large hands or an errant flick of the feather duster. As soon as I arrived in Gram's kitchen, I would assume my favorite position by climbing up on Grandpa's chair atop the Sears and Roebuck "booster" catalog, so I could reach whatever she would serve at the kitchen table.

I was deposited at my grandparents' house on weekday mornings before my parents went to work at 6:45 AM. I was promptly picked up every afternoon at 4:00 PM after my father got off day shift at the Naval Air Station in Alameda. Before he left for work at the railroad, my grandfather would have vacated his kitchen by 6:15 AM, being careful to top off his chair with the Sears catalog and a soft terrycloth dishtowel for me to sit upon.

Upon my arrival, my grandma would scoop me up in her arms, hug and kiss me and prop me up in the chair as she declared how much Spot had missed me during the night. Then she would carefully retrieve the gold jewelry box and pluck Spot from his "bed" of Kleenex and place the tiny canine in my four-year-old hands. It was the same routine each morning. I uttered the sincerest greetings, as if I hadn't seen him in years.

The mornings flew by as my grandma cooked breakfast and listened to me conduct personal interviews with Spot, asking what flavor of cake I should get for his birthday (chocolate is bad for dogs), if he wanted me to take him to see Santa Claus this year (Grandma could carry him in her purse), or if he liked plain or barbeque-flavored potato chips (BBQ, of course!)

During those years, my grandma heard *everything.* I thought she was smart, so I never wondered how she knew exactly what I liked. She possessed the sharpest hearing, despite the whirring eggbeaters, frying chicken, or the monotonous sound of the wringer washer. Somehow, she made sure I got the Betsy Wetsy doll, the farm set, and the Dale Evans costume I told Spot I just *had* to have! She always got it right because she listened well.

Spot was also the perfect student. I spent hours teaching him my favorite songs like, "How Much is that Doggie in the Window?" and "The Twelve Days of Christmas." It was very important not to skip or mix up a verse, because they all had to be in the right order to make sense. What happened if I made a mistake? I started over, of course—FROM THE BEGINNING! Grandma would just roll her eyes, as I emphasized to Spot, "It has to be perfect!"

After an entire day of conversation, singing, and an occasional popsicle or lemonade, it would be Spot's nap time. I would grab the Kleenex box and pull out enough tissues for Grandma to cushion Spot's bed for the evening. Before passing him off to Grandma, I would shower him with several wet kisses, tell him to remember to say his prayers, be a good boy, and goodnight.

Then Grandma would remove the booster catalog from Grandpa's chair, and we would happily do it all again the next day.

Silence
Loreen Barry

Silence, and a long, long look.

Pay attention at the crossroads,

And choose.

Enter the Mysterium.

The Trickster is here, holding the mirror, guarding the shadow.

Let go, laugh, and wait in bewilderment.

Don't reach and you will receive an enmeshment in woven water.

Transformation and then return.

Silence,

And a long, long look.

One Day
Ina Green

One day, the world stopped spinning—It just stopped turning. The ocean stopped in mid-wave, the birds seemed to be puppets suspended in the air.

You really couldn't tell that anything was different by looking at the mountains or the trees; they never moved anyway, but the color was gone. There were no rainbows.

What in the world made this happen? Literally, what, in the world, made it stop?

Well, it became known as "World Weary." The weight of the world just became too great to be able to withstand another rotation. Weighed down by the debris of eons of wars, greed, selfish interests, lies, passivity, man's inhumanity to man, to nature, to the planet. These are the obese weapons of mass destruction that have clogged the earth's core and shut down the world.

It seemed to be happening slowly, but the signs were there. Nobody paid attention to the creaks and moans. Nobody paid attention.

Nobody thought the system would ever be overtaken by the sludge and excessive weight heaped upon it.

But, one day, the world stopped spinning.

Simple Pleasures
Vicki Frink

I have discovered that I am a very tactile person, so it makes sense that one of my favorite simple pleasures focuses on touch.

For some reason, I love to pet dogs of almost any breed. Even if their fur is rough or extremely curly, running my fingers gently through the ruff is a delight for me—and generally for the dog, since I can usually sense if the animal is amenable to being petted.

And while I am a great fan of Amazon, I really prefer to shop for clothes in a brick-and-mortar store. There I can riffle through the racks, checking out the different fabric textures, whether it is the crispness of linen, the plushness of velvet, or the softness of bamboo. And silk—let's not forget silk, the *ne plus ultra* of fabrics. It whispers so seductively against my fingers that the hairs on my arms tingle gleefully.

But no touch is better or more gratifying than the skin of a loved one. I especially like the feet of babies, so malleable and fresh. Or the nape of my husband's neck, slightly damp and warm, throbbing with life.

Perhaps others might think my love of touch is a bit odd, or even (*shudder*) kinky, but the pleasure it gives both grounds and thrills me.

Something She Said
Susan Bono

"Something bad from something good," my Eastern European mother-in-law used to say in her heavily accented English. I knew she meant, "From something bad comes something good," but the words she left out made it sound like the opposite.

Now that she's been dead ten years, I've been thinking more about things I know about her life. WWII in Nazi-occupied Czechoslovakia. Her job in a German-run factory in Bratislava. Her schoolteacher boyfriend arrested and executed. The bombing. By the time she came to the United States at age twenty-nine, her country had been brutalized by Germany, starved by Churchill's blockade, bombed by the Americans, given to the Russians. She made the journey to the United States alone. "When I got off the boat in New York City," she told me once, "I didn't know one word of English, not even OK."

For over thirty years, my mother-in-law sent me affectionate cards and letters that were poetic, musical, and full of linguistic irregularities. They usually included money. She was a ceramics artist who always shared her earnings from the sales of her pots with her kids and grandkids. But while I appreciated her generosity and her sentiments back then, I always noticed her misspellings. I hope she never knew I silently corrected her grammar and made little jokes to my friends about her literary missteps. I rarely wondered how eloquently she might have expressed herself in her native language.

Now that it's too late, I wish I'd asked her more about her life, even though the past was something she never willingly spoke of. My husband has always insisted this was because of the war, but now I suspect she knew people would make assumptions, no matter what she said.

She had been poor. She raised her family in an affluent suburb of Los Angeles, but her childhood home had a dirt floor, and one of her first jobs in her rural village was herding geese. She'd wanted to be an actress, but her parents forced her to train as a seamstress. She arrived in America malnourished and lugging a big bag of goose down, the only thing of value her family could send with her. Shortly after she settled in New York City, she tore up her sewing certificate and got a job as a bookkeeper. She married a man whose family spoke Sicilian, one of five languages she had to learn in order to fit in.

Out in California, no one around her spoke Czech. She spent most of her life trying to communicate with people who couldn't really understand her, using languages that were always threatening to trip her up. She smiled and laughed often but had a hard time getting jokes. No one asked her how she managed to hold fast to her belief that every experience, no matter how terrible, eventually yields its gifts.

Now when I hear her voice in my head telling me, "Something bad from something good," I know I was the one who failed in translation. Now that it's too late, I long to make sense of the complex source text. Now that it's too late, I am learning to listen more carefully, and in the spaces between her words, my heart hears more of what she was trying to say.

First Love
Carole Williams

How did time go so fast? Yesterday we were a couple—well, not quite. In fact, it's been fifty-eight years since we broke up, but who's counting?

Geoffrey and I met in seventh grade and had an immediate, deep connection. It was as if we had known each other in another lifetime. I credit him with getting me through my turbulent, emotional adolescence. We were inseparable for nine years, even though we were always in different schools—until at some point in our junior year in college, when I stupidly encouraged a friend to go down to Princeton for a weekend in my place. I thought Geoffrey and I should date others before we married. Well, dammed if they didn't fall in love.

They married a few years later, and I married someone else, but that's another story. Both of us had children, and throughout those years, the four of us were friends. They were even my daughter's godparents. Our friendship survived their divorce, then mine, then both our remarriages. It survived, I suppose, because he always had a special place in my heart, the way best friends often do. I always admired his kindness, his ready smile, his creativity, his gentleness. We continued to bounce in and out of each other's lives, even after Richard and I left New York and moved to California in 1998.

At some point this past year, I heard through a mutual friend that Geoffrey had been diagnosed with a late-stage cancer, so I found some pictures of us, sent them, and he called. We talked for hours, and I believed him when he said that chemo would take care of the cancer.

A few months later, I woke up one early morning in a panic and thought, "I've got to email Geoffrey right this minute!" I ran to my computer, jotted off a "How-are-you-and-what-is-going-on" email. He didn't answer.

The next day, I got an email from his son saying that his father had passed away the day before. Then Geoffrey's wife called and said that she thought Geoff, or rather, his spirit, had visited me as he was dying, or just after he died, "to say goodbye."

If that's what prompted my panic, and I firmly believe it was, then I look forward to yet another lifetime with my soulmate, my friend of my heart. The time will go fast.

Twelve
Don Koss

Chapter 1

$$12:00$$

The following takes place between 12:00 and 1:00 AM

It was a dark and stormy night. A single light glows from the chateau atop the pine-studded hillside above the valley overlooking the winding stream below which curls its way through the shrub-lined banks of the rolling farmland that is the source of much of the food that supplies the nearby village which features what is said to be the absolute best pie shop in the state. John Holland is a very quiet, rather dull person. He sits alone in his pretentiously large and mostly empty country estate. He is waiting. Waiting for something to happen.

Chapter 2

```
1:00
```

The following takes place between 1:00 and 2:00 AM

Nothing happens.

Chapter 3

```
2:00
```

The following takes place between 2:00 and 3:00 AM

Sally Sommerton, a rather attractive and now very wealthy widow who inherited a tremendous fortune from her recently deceased husband, Cornwall, who passed away at the age of 95, is the closest neighbor of John Holland. Up until now, Sally and John have never met. It is said that Sally's deceased husband committed sexual suicide. Sally is 22. Word is that the funeral home charged an extra fee just to lessen the smile on Cornwall Sommerton's face. A pleasant, relaxed expression was appropriate, but the funeral home felt that the grin on Cornwall's face was a little too much.

Chapter 4

$$3:00$$

The following takes place between 3:00 and 4:00 AM

Chapter 4, you break up, but you give her just one more chance. *

Another old person joke. See music of the '50s and '60s.

Chapter 5

$$4:00$$

The following takes place between 4:00 and 5:00 AM

Sally has decided that she must meet John Holland. John, himself an extremely wealthy man, is living very nicely on the royalties he has been receiving from his tunnel in New York. He is able to trace his ancestors back to the 4th century and Hans the Dreary, who invented the country later known as "Hans," which was later changed to "Holland." Sally sits in the stillness with her pet Pomeranian, Porky.

"What shall we do, Porky?"

Porky growls. Porky hates that name.

Sally decides to throw a party. Little does she know where this decision will lead. She does have some very well-known friends whose attendance would add to the uppityness of any party. And uppityness is what she is going for. She pours herself another Gatorade and vodka and begins to make out a guest list.

Chapter 6

$$\boxed{5:00}$$

The following takes place between 5:00 and 6:00 AM

Her first thought is her old friend Dick Cheney. They aren't really close since that little business in the cloak room at the last White House Christmas party, but he had called her a couple of times from some undisclosed location, and in spite of what some might think, he is a party kind of guy. Not like his boss, who at her last party was found searching the house for what he called, "WMDs." Nobody knew what he was talking about.

Next on her list, Carlton J. Swinerton, the famous musician. (Her list isn't alphabetical). Carlton had been spending the last seven years in Tibet where he was working on a symphonic version of "Ding Dong, the Witch is Dead." He was almost done but had spent the last two-and-a-half years trying to decide how many trombones he should use. Common sense told him that 76 were too many, but he really liked trombones. And why did 76 sound so right?

Carlton J. Swinerton, Jr. is her next thought. Carlton, Jr., now living in England in the village of Ham-On-Wrye, is currently in a big legal battle trying to prove that he is in no way related to Carlton J. Swinerton.

Pierre LeBeouf would be a wonderful choice. The world-renowned chef has some free time. After inventing the peanut butter, mayonnaise, and onion sandwich, he opened a restaurant in New York City featuring his newest contribution to gastronomical pleasures. After three days, the restaurant closed, due to lack of interest. They had only one customer, a traveler from California who, along with his lawyer, claimed he had invented the peanut butter, mayonnaise, and onion sandwich and insisted that the sandwich be called "Don's Peanut Butter, Mayonnaise, and Onion Sandwich." Pierre refused, Don flew coach back to California, and the restaurant closed. It is now a combination Hooters and IHOP. The food's not great, but you gotta love the waitresses.

Clive Cussler is a thought. He probably wouldn't come, but he did like to see his name in print. (Maybe now he'll mention me in his next Dirk Pitt adventure. "Dirk, Al, and Don moved along the shadowy path towards the castle on the hill.")

Chapter 7

The following takes place between 6:00 and 7:00 AM

John Holland hasn't slept all night. He is wondering why Sally Sommerton has never invited him to a party. But he has other things on his mind. His uncle, Harry Holland–Aze, has recently passed away, and it is John's responsibility to arrange the services. Holland-Aze had recently been seeing an Asian foot therapist. He was so proud of his feet, which, at least in his opinion, were absolutely beautiful, that he wanted an open casket funeral. Only it was the bottom half of the casket he wanted open, with just his bare feet sticking out of the casket. Actually, not a bad idea. Harry Holland-Aze was a rather unattractive man.

Chapter 8

$$\boxed{7\!:\!00}$$

The following takes place between 7:00 and 8:00 AM

Sally's guest list is growing. Ricardo Mierda Gato was back in the country. He is the well-known writer of several children's books, the most successful being *Timmy the Turtle's Wild Adventure*. This is the story of a pet turtle whose owner, seven-year-old Willy Wanker, takes him on a family vacation. Along the way Timmy jumps out of the car and is lost. The story tells of his amazing adventures as Timmy finds his way over the 1½ miles back to his house. It takes 11 years.

Allan Treymaayne XXIII is her next thought. Besides having no idea of how to spell "Tremayne," the family throughout the years had absolutely no imagination when it came to naming their kids. Eleven of the Allan Treymaaynes were girls. Allen has just finished writing a musical about a cholera epidemic in the Congo. Broadway was abuzz over two of his big musical numbers, "Tut, Tut, Tsetse, Goodbye" and "E. Coli, My E. Coli".

Chapter 9

8:00

The following takes place between 8:00 and 9:00 AM

Somehow, probably through a White House leak, Phineas P. Sweatwell, the Council General of Slovenia, gets wind of the party and calls Sally to see what time it will start. Apparently, his invitation was lost in the mail. Sally informs him that the invitation wasn't lost and that he isn't on the guest list. It seems Sally cares not a lot for Phineas. She has a problem with anyone who thinks The Brothers Four were better than the Coachmen.

"You're a stench in the aroma of mankind," Sally tells Phineas.

Phineas spends all of Chapter 10 trying to figure out what the heck she is talking about.

Chapter 10

9:00

The following takes place between 9:00 and 10:00 AM

Phineas tries to figure out what the heck Sally means by "a stench on the aroma of mankind."

Chapter 11

$$10:00$$

The following takes place between 10:00 and 11:00 AM

The guest list is complete, the party is set. Everybody on the list is there. It is one of the best parties ever.

How everybody gets there by 10:00 in the morning, I have no idea.

John Holland isn't there. Sally forgot to invite him.

Chapter 12

$$11:00$$

The following takes place between 11:00 AM and 12:00 PM

It is the day after a dark and stormy night when a single light glowed from the chateau atop the pine-studded hillside above the valley overlooking the winding stream below which curls its way through the shrub-lined banks of the rolling farmland that is the source of much of the food that supplies the nearby village which features what is said to be the absolute best pie shop in the state. John Holland is still waiting for something to happen.

Nothing happens.

Epilog

The following takes place between 12:00 and 12:02 PM

John Holland, Sally Sommerton, Porky, Dick Cheney, Carlton J. Swinerton, Carlton J. Swinerton, Jr., Pierre LeBeouf, Clive Cussler, Ricardo Mierda Gato, Allan Treymaayne XXIII, Phineas P. Sweatwell, and yours truly all go to the bathroom.

Notes from the author:

The original title of this story was, "Twelve Hours in Mumbai." I was looking at the possibility of a 12-hour layover in Mumbai on the way home from India. As it turned out, our layover was much less than 12 hours, but my mind was already overflowing with the story you have just read. Was it the drugs, the Levoxyl, the Lipator? I had already stopped using Tums and Pepcid when I realized that my thinking that George Bush was president was just a dream.

Praise for "Twelve" by p.d. koss

"Another amazing novel from the fertile mind of one of the world's foremost unknowns."
p. d. koss

"Absolutely half as good as *24*."
Mary Lynn Rajskub, actor who plays Chloe O'Brian on 24

Look for *"Something Happens"*

p. d. koss's soon-to-be-released sequel to this exciting story. Read how he managed to maintain his esteemed position in the literary world.

Finality
Myrna Fleckles

Until I was in my early twenties, I had scrupulously avoided roller coasters. Ferris wheels were my go-tos at carnivals, and the bumper cars were best of all, but never, ever, roller coasters. Heights, dips, flimsy equipment, plus unsmooth motion on the edge of a seat definitely had no appeal!

In my twenties, however, I became more of a risk taker, so when two male friends from my boarding house in San Francisco suggested an evening at Playland at the Beach, I was up for it. It had not dawned on me that I might be given the opportunity to confront and conquer my disdain of roller coasters. Some power or other, however, thrust that golden opportunity onto my path that night, and I took the bait.

With a strong male companion holding onto his seat with one hand and me with the other, the journey began. Slowly, at first, then faster and bumpier, we sailed up and down steep slopes. I clutched my friend for dear life and yelled the whole way.

Never had I been so glad to have any "fun" end, as we slowed down and finally stopped. There was victory in the agony of having tried, but never repeated, just remembered.

The Big Fix
Hildy Williams

When it comes to broken stuff, I enjoy thinking outside the box. My repairs are generally unorthodox. They rarely require measuring or using a level. I keep a good supply of duct tape, gorilla tape, Velcro strips, wood glue, and old paint. Having spackle on hand is a must.

My longest project to date was from 1972—1979. Untrained and with no YouTube help, I decided to strip seventy years of paint layers off the Douglas fir paneling in our California Bungalow. The paneling was located throughout the downstairs, as well as around and over every doorway and window. I was able to track down a formula (which included lots of lye) for my stripper. Luckily, I was cautious enough to wear gloves and keep the doors and windows open while working. It was a long slow process but also very Zenlike and meditative. Bit by bit, the wood grain became dominant, and the painted wood became a memory.

We sold the house without any difficulty in 1980. I've always wondered if the new owners liked the house *in spite of* the natural wood paneling and thus set it right by repainting the paneling a trendy color of the time.

There is something to be said about jumping in, skilled or not, and tackling a project. I am not by nature a patient person. I want things done quickly. My home projects force me to slow down and just enjoy the process. Since moving to Varenna, my projects are much smaller, perhaps taking no more than five minutes or so. But I do love digging out my toolbox and getting my hands on those rolls of tape, paint, and Velcro!

Sergeant Crowell
Bill Ardizoia

If it moves, salute it. If it doesn't move, pick it up.
If you can't pick it up, paint it.
—Army maxim

There are people who leave an indelible mark on you as you go through life, like your mother and father, your brothers and sisters, your first love, and . . . your drill instructor.

We will keep the family and the first love stories in our pocket for the time being. Let me introduce you to my DI, Sergeant Crowell.

First, a little background. During my first two years of college, we were required to attend an ROTC course, complete with a weekly parade. The Army called it the Reserve Officers Training Course; we called it Rot-Cee. We would dress up in dull green dress uniforms, tan shirts, black ties, and round Army hats that looked like flying saucers on our heads. But it did give me experience in how to polish brass insignias and belt buckles on our uniforms and to put a spit-shine on our plain Army oxford shoes. This would come in handy later in my Army career.

Later, in May 1968, I joined the US Army Reserve, but was not able to immediately go to basic training. Most of the various training centers around the country at the time were filled to meet the needs of the conflict in Vietnam. In January 1969, I finally got my orders to proceed to the Reception Station at Fort Ord on the Monterey Peninsula for Basic Training. At the Reception Station, our group of future soldiers were assigned to one of five platoons, each with 48 men, which make up a company. I was in the Third Platoon, Charlie (or "C") Company.

This is where the story begins. I was lugging my duffle bag through the door of the barracks. Because I had spent over six months in weekend meetings with my reserve unit, I had been issued my Army clothing and was wearing my olive-drab fatigues, topped with my olive-drab baseball cap.

When a sergeant appears in the barracks, the usual notice is a shout of "At ease," as opposed to when an officer enters, when the shout is "Ten-hut," Army lingo for "Attention." Dutifully, when I saw a distinctive "campaign hat," approaching with what I believe was a person under it, I shouted, "At ease."

A massive hand then raised up and came down square on top of my head. I swear the thumb and little finger of the hand touched each ear. The hand then removed my Army baseball cap and shoved it into my chest.

"You don't wear your cover indoors, troop," the owner of the hand growled.

A couple of things were notable about this little incident. Most baseball caps have this little button on top made from metal covered in cloth. I am not sure of its purpose—it may be purely decorative, or it may hold the six or eight panels of the cap together. When the hand smacked me on top of my head to remove my "cover," it came down so hard, I think the button dented my skull. I think the dent on my head is still there to this day. It hurt like hell, making my eyes water. Army policy prohibits drill instructors, known as "DIs," to hit recruits, but since this DI, the owner of the hand, was technically adjusting my uniform, I guess the Army would have thought it was probably OK.

I took a step back and, through watery eyes, saw one of the most fearsome humans I have ever seen. I was reading Mark Twain's classic *Roughing It* at the time and in it, there was a beautifully described character by the name of Slade. The image of Slade immediately flashed through my mind. In the book, Slade was a frontier vigilante, who was, in Twain's words, an "actual ogre who, in fights and brawls and various ways, *had taken the lives of twenty-six human beings* [italics his]."

Twain went on to describe the fearsome character: "His face was rather broad across the cheek bones, and the cheek bones were low and the lips particularly thin and straight. But that was enough to leave something of an effect upon me, for since then I seldom see a face possessing those characteristics without fancying that *the owner of it is a dangerous man* [italics mine]."

In my mind, this DI's face was the image of Slade's combined with that of a pit bull. His cheek bones squeezed his eyes into slits that were too small for his face. I could not make out the color of his eyes, but I think they were yellow. All of this was topped with the "campaign hat." Civilians might call them "Smoky the Bear hats," "forest ranger hats," or "thumbtack hats." But, worn by a DI, the hat is their badge of office, their badge of honor, the symbol of authority. DIs never have to take them off while on duty, even in the chow hall. It was rumored that they may even wear them to bed.

This DI was about 6'2", tanned and weathered, lean and fit, with long, long arms ending in those abnormally big hands, which could cover my head. His knuckles were puffy, like half of a ping-pong ball under his skin. Were these the results of combat, barroom fights, or worse? His name tag on his stiffly starched uniform read "CROWELL."

That was probably the last time I looked at the face of Sergeant Crowell. If the DI caught you looking at him, he would immediately get in your face and scream, "You eyeballing me, boy?" The recruit would shout back, "NO,

Sergeant." Then, the DI would march off to terrorize some other small, shaved-head animal dressed in Army green.

The DI has absolute authority over recruits and their mission over eight weeks is to mold the platoon into a lean, mean, fighting machine. They control your life. They tell you when to get up, what you are going to do this day, when to eat, when to shower, and when to go to bed. We make no decisions—which is probably why some people like the military.

We learned to respect Sergeant Crowell, though it was probably more like we feared him. He wore various award tabs on his fatigues, including Combat Infantryman, Ranger, and Panama Jungle Training. We heard that he liked to go to the bars in Monterey and get into fights. He clearly had seen his share of action, both in and out of the military—and was here to give us the benefit of his experience. To be a DI, he had taken an oath to the Army to create discipline among the troops that he trained.

At the end of eight weeks, we received our individual orders to go to the next stage of Army training—Military Occupational Specialties—where soldiers learn to be truck drivers, cooks, radio operators, and all the things necessary by a functioning Army. I went with some of Charlie Company to Cook School at Fort Leonard Wood, Missouri.

I never saw most of Charlie Company again, including Sergeant Crowell. I'm sure he was assigned to the next group of raw recruits to mold into a lean, mean, fighting machine. Repeat, train, and train again.

Sometimes I am curious as to what happened to Sergeant Crowell. I'm sure he has retired from the Army, but I wonder if he still hangs out in Monterey, still brawling in bars, still denting people's skulls who are thoughtless enough to wear their caps indoors.

No Fish Fridays
Veronica Barclay

There were a lot of rules I had to follow growing up in the San Francisco Bay Area in the 1950s. My parents both worked, paid their bills on time, and were strong about defining rules for our family of three to live by. We were law-abiding citizens, helpful neighbors, and good Catholics.

Our Lady of the Rosary Catholic Church had just been built about two miles away from our new home. It boasted a large main church, a choir loft, complete with piano and organ, and a side chapel, also known as the crying room, which was specifically designed for loud infants or parishioners sneaking in late to services. Attached to the church building was a huge dining hall and kitchen, often used to accommodate weddings, Bingo, fund-raising activities, and Friday night dinners. This is where I learned to hate eating fish.

Since Catholics were not allowed to eat meat on Fridays, the church set up Friday night suppers for its parishioners. For $1.50 (75 cents for kids), church volunteers served a meatless family meal. Fish sticks or meatless spaghetti, the menu NEVER changed. You could have your choice of oven-baked frozen (soggy) fish sticks or meatless (watery) spaghetti, served with a side of green salad and Wishbone Italian dressing, and one slice of over-toasted (burnt) garlic bread.

These Friday night church dinners are where I honed my negotiating skills. Because I despised both entrees, I would take my loaded first serving directly to the biggest kid at the end of the line and offer to trade a fish stick in exchange for his burnt garlic bread or my watery spaghetti for salad. Then I would go back in the food line for more salad and burnt bread until I was full.

My parents got tired of fighting the Friday night traffic in order to get to the church before the dinner was over. About that time, my dad switched to working the swing shift at the Naval Air Station. When he started getting paid every other Friday, we replaced the Friday night routine with an every-other-Saturday-night pizza party at La Hal's Pizza Parlor, often inviting a relative or friend to join us. There, we enjoyed a large cheese pizza, unlimited Caesar salad, garlic bread, and a glass of bubbles (beer for the adults and a Coke for me.)

I loved La Hal's Pizza nights but learned to hate those alternate "no paycheck this week" Fridays. That's when my mom would break out the box of Morton's Frozen Fish Sticks and turn on the oven to heat them up. Oh no! Not again!

We had a rule in our house. You could not leave the table until you ate all your dinner. Remember the starving children in China and Africa? With no other kid or even a dog to help bail me out of these Friday night predicaments, I had to learn to stand up for myself. Don't back down. A big realization for a grade schooler. But it was necessary.

My mother could buy fresh fish from the meat market or grocery store, but as much as she liked to order it when we went to a special occasion restaurant, she rarely made it at home. It was always a disaster. That's because she would hover over the blue Styrofoam trays of cleaned fish fillets in the Lucky supermarket before finally taking one to the cashier to pay the exorbitant price for it. She would proudly trot home with her selected treasure and quickly deposit it in the refrigerator meat tray, where it would reside for the next three to five days before she would remember to cook it. Of course, by then it would have commenced stinking up everything in our refrigerator, even before she got it anywhere near a frying pan. When it was finally cooking, the smell of old fish would permeate the house, garage, and front yard, no matter how long she kept a lid on it. It got so bad I would throw up every single time my mom fried fish in our house.

You would have thought she could have figured this out. Nope. On those meatless Friday nights when she had no eggs or cheese available, my mom would set me in my chair at the kitchen table and plop two baked fish sticks on a plate along with a tablespoon of ketchup.

It stunk! I would feel my stomach grumbling, rub my teeth with a finger full of ketchup, and swing my feet back and forth to try and trick my brain. Every twenty minutes or so, my mother would come by the table to see how much I had eaten. She sucked her teeth and reminded me of the starving children, waiting homework, no dessert or cartoons. Eventually, she would go into her bedroom and fall asleep. Then I would fall fast asleep with arms and legs crossed in my booster chair and my head drooping on my chest with my plate full of fish sticks and half-eaten ketchup in front of me.

My fish sticks were the perfect midnight snack for my dad when he came home from work. In one quick swipe, he slid both fish sticks through the remaining ketchup and popped them into his mouth in about five seconds flat. One or two swipes with a napkin later, he would scoop his daughter into his arms and tuck her in bed, clothes and all.

To this day, I still don't eat fish!

My Acting Debut
Carole Williams

Does everyone have memories that give them nightmares? One of mine took place on the stage of my elementary school. I was in eighth grade, just thirteen, when the Spring play was announced. It was to be *Arsenic and Old Lace*, and I really, really wanted to be in it. I hoped Mr. Kaye, our drama teacher, would give me the part of the ingenue, Elaine. I actually thought I'd get it, but was passed over in favor of my friend, Pam. I was devastated but tried only to show that I was pleased for her.

Pam went to all the rehearsals, memorized her whole part. Two weeks before the performance, we decided to go practice for the end-of-the-year track and field competition. We were alone on the field at the high jump, and she asked me to teach her how to do the "Western Roll." Instead of scissoring your legs over the bamboo bar, you throw your body over, back first, then kick your legs in the air to get them over, landing on your back. I demonstrated, and then it was her turn.

She tried it, and when she landed, I heard the pole break. I remember thinking that I never would have guessed that it was possible to break a piece of bamboo that was more than an inch thick. When I turned around, she was looking at her arm in disbelief. That loud snap wasn't the pole. That was Pam's arm! It was grossly misshapen. She was in shock.

It felt as though it took forever for me to get someone to help, but Pam was finally carted off in an ambulance. It was my fault, and to make matters even worse, Mr. Kaye gave me her part in the play. I managed to learn the lines, the rehearsals were okay, but the performance—well, that was something else.

Eric, my fiancé in the play, was in my class. We had never rehearsed our passionate embrace and kiss in the second act, which turned out to be a bad call on Mr. Kaye's part. The only experience I'd had was a kiss playing Spin the Bottle, not nearly enough preparation. When we got to the kiss that fateful Saturday night, the whole school erupted in cheers and screams, and I, nervous and ashamed, started to laugh. And laugh. I could not stop. Eric took my shoulders in his hands and shook me. Nothing worked. Mercifully, someone finally dropped the curtain so I could compose myself, which I finally did.

Unfortunately, we'd lost the rhythm and the chain of events and managed to jump into dialog that belonged in the third act. Down the curtain went—again. To this day, I cannot remember whether that, too, was my fault. But I do remember that Mr. Kaye was so furious that his face was beet red. After the end of the school year, none of us ever saw him again.

The good news: I never tried out for a play again, and to my knowledge, never caused another teacher to quit teaching.

The Pagoda
Nancy Humphriss

When I was eight and my sister, Shirley, was eleven, we were living in Northampton, Massachusetts, with my parents. It was 1939, and the much advertised and anticipated New York City World's Fair had just opened. It was to be one of the biggest and most expensive fairs ever. We heard the slogan, "Dawn of a New Day," every day on the radio, and exhibits were to be based on the future. Something called "television" would be introduced.

At dinner that night, my mother told me that she, her best friend, and Shirley were going, leaving me home with my father. I, of course, reacted with tears, cries of "Not fair!" and promises to behave, etc. Nothing would change my mother's mind. She tried to explain that I was too young to understand all the exhibits and would get too tired. My dad, who was my favorite person in the world, took me aside, assuring me that he would find something special we could do together. While being left behind still stung, this promise helped some.

The next day, he invited my best friend, Lois, who lived across the street, to come with us to Look Park, a place I loved to go. It had a swimming pool with a shallow end for children, swings, see-saws, slides, and a merry-go-round. We sat at a picnic table to eat our lunch. Peanut butter and jelly, of course, with milk and cookies. A perfect day!

At home for dinner later, my dad made my favorite: blueberry pancakes with butter and maple syrup. I'd had this treat only for breakfast before, never for dinner!

The next morning, we went downtown to Northampton, first to the library, where I chose two books to borrow, then to lunch for a hot dog, and finally, to the bookstore, where I was allowed to pick out two more books to buy and take home. The evening was spent reading one of my new books with my dad.

The last day was spent playing with Lois, mostly having a tea party at her house, using a small table with Lois's real ceramic cups and saucers, real tea, and cookies. But the special event was saved for dinner, just my dad and me.

Northampton was anything but ethnically diverse. There were no Black, Asian, or Hispanic people, and only an occasional French Canadian. So when my father said we were going to a new restaurant in town, called The Pagoda, to have Chinese food, I didn't know what to expect. He said it was located a short distance from Main Street, and very popular. Even former President Calvin Coolidge occasionally walked over from his law office to have lunch.

Dad had made a reservation , so when we walked in, we were greeted by the owners, Mr. and Mrs. Mei Chang. They said hello to us and showed us to our seats, handing a menu to my father. My eyes were locked on the ceiling, where red and gold paper lanterns hung in bright display, with accompanying ribbons as well. Strange-to-my-ears music was playing, and I didn't recognize the sounds.

Dad showed me the menu, trying to explain basic things. He said he would order for us. I noticed there was no silverware and watched other diners using some long wooden sticks, which seemed to get the food in their mouths somehow. Soon hot tea was set before us, which I tasted, finding it good.

My father chose food he knew wouldn't be too unusual for me to eat: Chicken Chow Mein; delicious noodles with a tangy sauce; fried rice with shrimp; and egg rolls, crispy and dipped in a black sauce—soy sauce, my father called it. My only problem was I couldn't use the long wooden sticks at all. Of course, my dad asked for a fork for me, and then I could eat.

I loved every minute of this new eating experience, and I quickly discovered I loved Chinese food! The dessert wasn't very tasty, but it was fun—a hard piece of something encasing a bit of paper. On the paper was a written fortune, telling me what my future held: happiness and success, of course! All these memories are still indelible in my mind, everything from the food to the smells, the music, and especially the bright lanterns filling the ceiling.

After we got home it was bath time, followed by a story. "What should I read you tonight?" asked my father. To end a perfect day, it must be a perfect book. *Winnie the Pooh*, of course! The chapter about Eeyore and Piglet.

The next day my mother and Shirley returned, bringing us many fascinating stories about The World's Fair. My mother was amazed at being able to see and hear President Roosevelt deliver a speech to Congress to an audience there in New York. Television was going to change our lives, for sure.

Shirley couldn't stop talking about the exciting ride on the latest Ferris Wheel midway at the fair's midway. I was happy with the tiny ceramic doll with her own bed they brought for me. But all in all, I felt I had the best time being with my dad and having the new experience of Chinese food at The Pagoda.

The Plot
Nancy Parsons

Kate was sick! She was really ill, and it was Spring planting time for our garden plots on the northwest side of the Big House. (Since we reside in a Senior Living Community, we have been instructed not to refer to them as plots, so henceforth, in this true story, our plots will be called garden beds.)

I knew that Kate would recover, but by the time that happened, and she was strong enough to walk up and over the hill to her bed, it would probably be too late in the season to plant seeds or dig in tomato starts or place cucumbers and tender herbs. Since I love to visit nurseries, shop for plants, and tend gardens, I volunteered to plant Kate's bed for her. By the time she felt stronger, the flowers and veggies would be settled in and well on their way to maturity, and the only tasks that Kate would need to do were a little weeding and harvesting the crops.

It was a great plan but so difficult to implement. The earth in Kate's bed was compacted and full of weeds. It desperately needed a strong, younger person to dig it up and amend the soil. Plus, the water drip lines needed to be repaired, so I really needed an expert from the garden crew.

I placed a work order, and then I waited, and waited, and waited. I talked to many folks about getting help, but none appeared. Meanwhile, Spring was coming, slowly, but still coming!

May 1st arrived and still no help. It was the day of the management turnover and there was a gathering in the Livingroom. I was about to join the festivities when I saw Jenny standing near her office door. I gave my spiel for "Help!" to one more person, one more time. She referred me to the new concierge to place yet another order.

The concierge was a new young woman trying her best to hold everything together in the midst of all the noise and activities surrounding her. She was quite busy answering questions and directing lots of folks who were constantly passing by her desk.

When she had a free minute, I asked her if she could place a work order for me. She was quite willing to do so, but was a bit handicapped because the Internet was down! She managed to find a pencil and a recycled brown paper bag and started to take notes to Dan for a work order.

Our conversation went as follows:

"My name is Nancy Parsons. I live in a casita at 1415 Fountaingrove. My next-door neighbor at 1411, Kate Van Ness, is ill and she needs her garden bed, number 22, turned over."

For some reason, I thought it best to ask her to repeat what she wrote. Here is her reply:

"Nancy Parsons who lives at 1415 and is a friend of Kate Van Ness who lives at 1411 and is sick requests that someone go to her house and turn over her mattress."

Another Day, it's a Doctor Dey
Don Koss

Friday, July 9, 2021. I'm scheduled for a battery replacement in my pacemaker. It's clear skies and a warm morning, almost 70° by 8:00 a.m. We're expecting low 90's today. I take my "Pre-Surgery CHG body cleansing shower." With clean clothes and cleansed body, I'm now ready to go. At around 10:00 a.m., we will head for Marin General Hospital.

We're at MGH at 10:20. We check in at the Main Entrance and they send us up to Pre-Registration. I fill out the forms I was told in a telephone call the previous day that I would not have to fill out because they were taking the information over the phone. Oh, well.

A few minutes there and we move on to another office. We get a little lost wandering the halls of the newly huge Marin General. We get some help from a gentleman wearing scrubs. He could be anybody—from a surgeon to a nurse to an escaped psycho patient. What matters is he used to be a guide at Yellowstone Park, so he knows how to show people around.

Now we take another seat for a few minutes, and I continue answering the questions: Name? Birthdate? They check my weight, and they believe me when I tell them my height is 5'7."

From here we are taken to a room where I will wait until surgery time. It's now 10:45. It's a single bed room with a chair by the window where Roberta can sit and wish she had brought a book. The nurse hands me a smock and says I can just take off my shirt and leave my shorts on. I put on the smock (or is it a gown?) and lie down on the bed.

The surgery, or, as we like to call it, "the procedure," is scheduled for 12:30, so I know we have some time before we go. This time will be spent hooking me up to some kind of drip. The entry point on my body is the top of my left hand, and it's a little uncomfortable. I'm hoping this is as uncomfortable as I will be for the rest of the day.

Another nurse comes in and announces she will be removing chest hair that I have been growing for several years now. She takes out her little electric shaver and off she goes. A minute or so into the effort, she quietly says, "*Oops.*"

I look at her and say, "You know.... If there's one word I don't like to hear in a hospital, it's '*Oops.*'"

That got a good laugh out of her and the nurse entering information on the computer.

"How did it go at the hospital yesterday?"

"I'm not sure. Somebody said, *"Oops,"* and I passed out."

Just another fun day at the hospital.

Roberta really wishes she had brought a book.

At 12:20, they hook up another fluid that will be pumped into me. They tell me someone will be here in twenty minutes to move me to surgery. Meanwhile, Roberta now has the information she needs to pick me up later and she can depart.

Twenty minutes becomes an hour when, at 12:30, a nurse comes in to move me to the Procedure Room. I tell her I'm still wearing my shorts, and is that OK? She has no problem with that, but she suggests I change my socks.

She maneuvers the narrow, rolling bed out the door and down the hallway. We roll to a stop outside a room with a sign over the entrance telling me this is the Procedure Room. Now wearing my hospital issued, non-slip socks, they have me walk about twenty feet from my rolling bed into the Procedure Room. With a little help and a step stool, I climb onto the table where I will spend the next couple of hours. We spend the next twenty minutes or so prepping for the actual procedure. During this time Dr. Dey arrives, and we have a little chat.

Sujoya Dey, MD, FACC, makes you feel comfortable from her first words. FACC is Fellow of the American College of Cardiology. She is a graduate of Stanford Medical School, so we don't discuss my one year at Cal. There's nothing like a surgeon who looks younger than your granddaughter. She lifts the sheet covering my chest and says, "Oh, that looks fine."

I tell her I'm glad to hear that. I would have been a little worried if she had said it looked really bad, or even not so good. She agrees. She then tells me what the procedure today will entail. They might even replace the whole pacemaker. They will decide when they get a look at everything.

I have a question. "Did I hear you say, 'local'?" I was kind of planning on getting some sleep while this was going on.

She confirms that it will be a local but that I will be "*very* relaxed."

Someone suggests we remove my belt. Something about the metal buckle touching my skin. I have no idea why that's a problem. Maybe something about electrical things happening to your body during operations? The cell phone in my pocket doesn't bother them. I guess as long as it doesn't ring during the procedure. I'm pretty sure it's turned off.

A nurse informs me that Dr. Dey is the only one allowed to do the surgery, and to prevent me from trying to assist, they will lash my hands firmly to the table.

Now I'm a little more concerned. What are they going to do that I might want to strike out and do some damage? And what if my nose itches?

One of the nurses scrubs down the work area on my now hairless chest, and they mark the outline of my pacemaker. It's very visible and easy to see. I hear people talking.

Nurse Number 1: "What are we doing today?"

Nurse Number 2: "Something about one of those heart things."

Number 1: "You mean Pacemaker?"

Number 2: "Yeh. I think that's what they're called."

Number 1: "OK. I'll Google it. Pacemaker? Is that one word?"

Number 2: "No idea. Just type in *p, a, c, e,* and something should come up."

Number 1: "I've got it. There are a couple of YouTube videos. What are we looking for?"

Number 2: "Hang on. Let me check. It's written down here somewhere. OK. Here it is. Battery replacement. Evidently, they have little batteries in them. I think I saw some batteries in a drawer over in that table."

Number 1: "There are three videos on Pacemaker battery replacement."

Number 2: "Just pick the shortest one and we'll take a look at it. This shouldn't take long."

Number 1: "Hang on. Here's Dr. Dey. Maybe she knows how to do this."

That's the last thing I remember.

I will have to say I do feel the injection when they numb my chest, but I've certainly felt worse. Probably at the dentist. I would suggest if you are ever in pain, just think of the dentist, and you'll realize whatever's happening now isn't so bad.

I can hear Dr Dey and whoever is assisting her. The assistant might be the fellow from St Jude, the manufacturer of the Pacemaker. Among other subjects, they are discussing some new movies coming out. I have a sheet tented over my head, so I can't see what's going on. I figure that's a good thing. One of them asks how I'm doing.

"I'm fine, but I have to tell you, I hear *Black Widow* (the new movie with Scarlett Johansson) isn't that good."

They are disappointed but appreciative of my report.

And they're done. They take the sheets off my head and chest, add some elastic tape to hold down and protect the bandages over the new incision, and send me home.

Well, not directly home. They slide me off the table onto a gurney and wheel me to a recovery room. It's 3:00. I'll rest here for about half an hour. I have a couple glasses of water and a couple of Tylenol, just in case. I'm not feeling any discomfort right now, but we figure a little preventative dose won't hurt. Both Dr. Dey and the recovery room nurse have called Roberta, and she, along with one of our daughters, Darcy, are already on their way here.

At 3:30 the nurse wheelchairs me down to the main entrance where Roberta is waiting. I climb into the car, and we head for home.

Darcy stays and we chat a while. Part of it about Sunday and her birthday. To aid in my recovery, I will have a Jack Rudy gin and tonic. The Jack Rudy and soda water are the tonic part. 24 is the gin part. I feel better already.

I haven't eaten since last night, so I'm ready for dinner. Roberta's chicken tetrazzini and a few glasses of wine do the job.

Although I napped on and off at the hospital, I have no trouble getting to sleep around 10:00 p.m. I sleep pretty well, even though I have to stay on one side. It's a fairly warm night, so we not only have the window open, we have the fan running, too. It's going to be hot. We expect mid 90's and maybe even higher.

The next day, I seem to have a little problem that might be due to some of yesterday's meds. It seems I'm running quite frequently to the bathroom. It's more of a nuisance than anything. I tell Roberta that I might have to think about our regular Saturday dinner out plans. She is just back from getting her hair done and is sitting at her computer.

"I think we might want to wait until later today to decide if I can go anywhere for dinner."

"OK. No problem," she answers. She took that really well. "I'll bring you back something."

I knew I could count on her.

Haiku
Loreen Barry

Windy Day

Oh, windy day!
A leaf, like a little bird,
Leaps onto my pathway.

Season's Wall

Behind Season's Wall
Lies the Ragweed's Seed of Tao,
Everspring of Life.

The Care & Feeding of Hobos
Veronica Barclay

According to my grandmother, I come from a long line of hobo lovers. My grandpa worked for the Southern Pacific Railroad in Barstow, California, so he was constantly bringing a stranger or coworker home for lunch or dinner. It was never a problem for my grandma, who would joke that she could always add another stone to that night's soup, as she diced up an extra carrot or potato to add to the meal she was preparing.

I'm sure I developed my habit of picking up "strays" from her, based on the countless homeless animals and holiday "orphans" I would befriend or bring home. As a young girl, I watched my grandma care for injured birds, stray cats, and junkyard dogs, but she never gave me lessons on the care and feeding of hobos. That's something I learned in The School of Not-So-Hard Knocks from Hobo Chuck.

Chuck was a real hobo living on the train tracks along Pier 26 in San Francisco. He shared a boxcar with a couple of other transients who were able to secure day jobs or weeklong projects in exchange for cash, meals, or "trade goods," like clothes, alcohol, or cigarettes. Wherever that boxcar was parked, Hobo Chuck walked to our pier offices every morning to turn on the heat and start the coffee before any of the other employees arrived. Then, he would flick on the radio and leaf through the *San Francisco Chronicle* before zipping on his one-piece, dark gray work overalls and baseball cap—his daily uniform—just before 7:30 AM.

That's when the rest of us would show up for our 8-5 shifts at Yobo Imports—a San Francisco-based, hand-painted tee shirt importer. The company consisted of two owners, a warehouseman, an office manager, an accountant, and an office secretary (me.) Occasionally, we would hire day laborers from the hobos that hung around the pier early in the mornings. That's where they found Chuck.

He was not what I thought a hobo would look like. Hobo Chuck was about forty-five, clean-shaven, with a crew cut, and a calm demeanor, and he embraced whatever menial or dirty task was thrown his way. He was friendly to his coworkers and dock union workers, even though they made more than his $2.25 per hour. On breaks, I would sometimes sit at the end of the pier to watch the seals and get some fresh air. That's when Chuck would stop by on the forklift.

Our fifteen-minute-break chats revealed he was from Nebraska, had two sisters somewhere in the Midwest, was unmarried, and thought San Francisco hippies were too touchy feely for him. He loved Dungeness crab, California weather, and Tony Bennett. San Francisco seemed like the perfect landing spot for him.

Every Friday at exactly 4:45 PM, after most of the office staff left early to beat the Friday afternoon traffic, Hobo Chuck would climb the warehouse stairs to our office to retrieve his "hanger" from the coat closet. That's where he kept his Night on the Town brown wool sportscoat, white shirt, clean jeans, and brown wool necktie. The Ladies Room, with the tiny corner sink and huge wall mirror, was perfect for washing off a week's worth of dust and grime before his obligatory splash of Hai Karate men's cologne. With a final glance in the mirror, he carefully parted his way-too-short bangs to one side before stashing his work overalls under the sink and heading toward the door. At exactly 4:55, he would say goodnight to me in the hallway before heading for the stairs and his night out.

Over the months to come, I noticed buttons missing from Chuck's "night out" coat, so I bought a new matching set and sewed them on. Another time, I took his white shirt to the Chinese laundry around the corner from our office and had it cleaned and pressed with extra starch. Chuck strutted out the door that Friday night like a proud rooster. I never told him I did these things, and he never asked about them, but I'm sure he knew.

Coming from the Midwest, he had never tasted avocados or alfalfa sprouts until I shared a sandwich with him from Avocado Al's. Made with half an avocado and anchored with cream cheese, sliced tomatoes, olives, freshly cut alfalfa sprouts, and ranch dressing atop homemade ten-grain wheat bread, this sandwich turned a lifelong beefeater into a west coast vegetarian. At Christmas that year, I sprouted some alfalfa seeds in my kitchen between damp paper towels and painstakingly transplanted them into a pint of garden soil in a canning jar. I wrapped a red ribbon around the top, and with care and watering instructions, including the suggestion to put them on his windowsill, I left it by his hanger in the coat closet one Friday night.

Of course, in usual Chuck fashion, he never said anything. And, of course, I didn't ask.

It never occurred to me back then that hobos don't have windowsills.

The Changing View
Susan Bono

For Gerald Haslam (1937-2021)

One overcast, chilly morning in April of 2022, I was staying close to the heater in my office, so when I heard a woodchipper start up somewhere on our street, I didn't go outside to investigate. Instead, I went back to reading an email from the widow of my writing mentor, Gerald Haslam, who had died the year before. Jan was trying to work around the stormy weather front that was forcing her to move Gerry's upcoming outdoor memorial on the Sonoma State campus under cover. We'd been praying all winter for rain in drought-ravaged California, and here we were, in April, getting more than we asked for.

The next message in my inbox explained the infernal noise. It was from Melissa, across the street and down the hill a little, informing her neighbors that the old, ailing magnolia tree in their backyard was being removed. She expressed deep sorrow at the impending loss and invited us to pay our respects to a Wallace Court resident that had been around longer than any of us. I wondered if her magnolia was the same age as our pepper tree, the one I worry about every time the wind picks up. The pepper tree must have been planted shortly after our house was built in 1939, because it was already huge and nearly hollow when my husband and I arrived in 1981. These two trees are among several on this block reaching the end of their lifespans. That is the way of things, but yesterday, I couldn't bear watching one of them being turned into sawdust.

The next morning, when I stepped out front to get my newspaper, the neighborhood seemed different. Did Melissa's yellow house look a little lighter and livelier without the weighty backdrop of the aged tree, or was it just the effect of a newly washed April sky after a night of rain? Perhaps my view of the distant hills had widened a little, but I didn't have a mental "before" picture to consult, so I really couldn't tell.

I didn't feel sad, exactly, but I wished I'd paid more attention, gotten to know the magnolia better. I feel the same about other trees in my life: the apricot in my childhood backyard, the valley oaks dotting the Dingle school playground, the mysterious palms lining the Woodland library walkway. I'm grateful for my fragmented memories of bark, leaves, nuts, and fruit, but there is so much I will never know about them, including why they keep visiting me in reverie. I can only hope I'll remember the sound of whispering leaves, the scratch of bark under my hand, the feel of a ripe apricot pulling free from its branch.

It's the same with Gerry. I'll never forget how grateful I was to be sitting in his writing class at Sonoma State the year I turned forty. A decade earlier, I'd left a teaching career to stay home with our sons. They no longer needed me in the same way, and I felt like I'd lost my purpose. For one semester I flourished under Gerry's protective shade, and it was there I began sprouting ideas of my own about writing and becoming a small press publisher.

I loved Gerry's stories about Bakersfield and Oildale. They helped me reclaim my Central Valley roots. I took courage when he said things like, "It's not so much about talent, it's more about persistence." My favorite advice of his was, "When writing memoir, I recommend getting as close to the edge of fiction as you can without falling in." I've shared his comments with other writers so often over the years, they almost feel like my own.

When the class ended, I started a personal essay journal and Gerry retired. Over the next quarter of a century, he never missed an opportunity to praise my writing or boost my magazine, and whenever our paths crossed at our local bookstore, he let me know he was happy to see me. We exchanged occasional notes and email. I have saved some of his messages, and looking at them recently, I was surprised by how encouraging they were. Back then, I hadn't really registered how supportive he was, how much time he, a prolific and highly regarded writer, made for me. Now he's gone, and things look different in ways I can't quite put my finger on.

The freshness of the morning air gave me hope that the weather might clear for the next day's memorial. When I returned to Gerry's beloved campus, I would be walking under the canopy of trees he had seen when they were newly planted fifty years ago. I squinted in the direction of that missing magnolia and thought about all the things that continue to abide, even in their absence.

Windows of Wisdom
Nikki King

These were my late-night thoughts from years ago:

As F. Scott Fitzgerald said, "In a real dark night of the soul, it is always three o'clock in the morning, day after day." I wouldn't exactly say I'm having a dark night of my soul, but I do often wake up and have a hard time falling back to sleep. I try to think about the happenings of the day with the aim of putting a positive spin on its events. I wonder, "What did I accomplish today or who did I enjoy seeing or conversing with?"

But then negative thoughts usually push their way in, and I remember times when I misspoke or was too loud or blundered in some way. Suddenly, all the negative or unpleasant things come to mind, even going back to my childhood.

Then and there, I command myself to stop and think only of the positive aspects of my rather eventful life. It has always been harder to credit myself with my positive life events. To calm myself, I often recite Robert Frost's poem, "Stopping by Woods on a Snowy Evening."

Happily, over the years, I have developed a positive state of mind and vanished negativity from my life here at Varenna. I look forward to every day and count my blessings.

James
Bill Ardizoia

*All stories, if continued far enough, end in death, and he is
no true storyteller who would keep that from you.*
—Ernest Hemingway

Doctor Death paid a visit last week, as always, without warning. I got notice via email that the Doctor had left with one soul.

James was a born and bred Texan. He was a graduate of the University of Texas at Arlington, which is the little institutional brother of *Thee* University of Texas, as they call it down there.

I first met James when he walked into a conference room at the Bank of America world headquarters in San Francisco, where we were both working at the time. I thought I was looking in the mirror. He was bald like me; he had a beard like me; he wore a suit with a vest like me. The only thing that was different was that he spoke with a Texas accent.

He was the ultimate Texan. Is there any other kind? He always had a smile and a quick laugh. His darting eyes were always looking for the next good time, and he always seemed to have everything under control. Beer was his middle name, as was mine. Because of the physical likeness, as well as our taste in beverages, we were immediately attracted to each other.

Over the years, we both worked hard and partied harder. Lots of guy stuff: ball games—A's, Giants, and 49ers; Friday night gatherings at various saloons in San Francisco's financial district; company softball teams.

The name of our softball team was the MCPs, or Male Chauvinist Pigs—which, incidentally, we were not—but the term was popular with certain segments of the population at the time. Our team featured Lester, our pitcher from Hawai'i, whose "Spam ball" was found extremely tasty by opposing batters who feasted on it with hit after hit. Our team finished in the bottom of the league standings, outscored by a wide margin. Our team was so bad, in fact, that I decided to set fire to my team shirt on the backstop after our last game so that no one would ever have to endure the disgrace of having to wear it again. James told me he thought it was the funniest thing he had ever seen.

I received notice of Doctor Death's visit via a photo of James with an attractive lady who I later found out was his lovely granddaughter. At first glance, I thought he had joined up with a sweet young thing, which would not have surprised me. James always had an eye for the younger ladies, and they for him. Women were attracted to his devilish grin and easy laugh, more like a giggle.

One of his girlfriends worked at a local bank. We called her Luscious Lynn. Their mutual attraction was apparent from day one. The relationship, like most of them, was like a bonfire of shredded paper—when lit, it was quick to turn into a blaze, and then, *poof*, it was out. All that was left were a few charred pieces, maybe memories of their sweeter moments, being carried away by the breeze.

James became a legend among our group. My friend, Pat H. tells the story of the time he and James worked at a bank located on an Indian reservation up in Humboldt County. Pat and James went to the local bar for lunch, where they had a few beers. When playing pool with some of the locals, a dispute started, and they almost got drilled with cue sticks by some of the citizens. Pat said they were lucky to get out alive. They flew out of the bar, jumped in their car, laid some rubber, and laughed all the way back to Eureka.

James met up with another colleague, Paul F., and the two of them were fabulous to be around. They were inseparable. They finished each other's jokes, were always up for a good time, and lived by the old adage, "Never let the fear of striking out keep you from playing the game." Paul changed jobs a few years later and got married. As true friends, they stuck together until Paul got the Big C and passed away a few years later.

James was a true Texan and I was not surprised when he said he was leaving California and moving back. I never knew the real reason. It seems that most ex-pats from Texas eventually return like homing pigeons on a mission from God.

We last got together in person in Dallas earlier in the 2000s when I was attending a professional business conference. I believe James was in real estate at the time. We met up and James guided me, not surprisingly, to a couple of places, which down there they call "gentlemen's clubs." The only gentlemen I saw were a couple of off-duty Texas A&M football players stuffed into tuxedos. The outfits no doubt gave an air of respectability to the establishment, at least it did for me. Right.

James gave me a call a couple of years ago when he moved to Tahoe—I forget where exactly, maybe Incline Village. He said he was going to come down to the Wine Country at some point, but never did. This may have been one of those "to-do" list things that you know you want to do, but something always seems to take priority. Until it is too late to make the call. Kind of lost track of him after that.

I do have one of James' old email messages where he said, "I tell a lot of California stories here in Texas and Paul and you and the others are in most of them. My time in San Francisco was some of the best years of my life and I remember all the guys." I guess he forgot about the ladies.

Remaining in the Bud
Ina Green

No risk, no fear of failure
never showing who you really are
the duckling or the swan
never having to show your face.

What a small world
No bees bussing around, no sun breathing you open
no signs of admiration for your real beauty.

The time warp of blossoming shows petals and pistils
and everything else that makes you a flower
the miracle of what was locked inside the bud.

Yes, worth blossoming even for a short time
even when the petals dry up and fall.

What can compare to the experience of growth
and becoming
even for a short time.

Goals for Aging
Myrna Fleckles

Be graciously old,
Not grumpily elderly.
Complaints not welcome.

Be self-aware old.
Forego much that used to be.
Embrace parts of now.

Be forgiving old.
Use wisdom gained, overlook.
Throw away grudges.

Be quietly old.
Listen more, speak less, be calm.
Respect your instincts.

Be old and content.
Do not surrender values.
They are who you are.

Inside each of us is a natural-born storyteller,
waiting to be released.
Robin Moore

AUTHOR BIOS

 **Bill Ardizoia** was born in San Francisco to immigrants from Italy and learned to speak English after attending grammar school. He attended Riordan High School, Santa Clara University, and George Washington University. His business career includes periods as regulator with the US Treasury Department, as a senior manager with major banks, and as a consultant and Firm Director with Deloitte & Touche. He has lived in Sonoma County for over 20 years. His favorite quote is from author Tom Robbins: "There is no such thing as a weird human being. It's just that some people require more understanding than others."

 **Veronica Barclay** was born and raised in the San Francisco Bay Area. She and her husband, Mark, met at college and have been married almost 50 years. They embarked on social work careers before moving to Mendocino County, where she worked as a horseshoer and managed an exotic animal ranch. In 1980, they moved to Sonoma and Napa Counties, where Veronica began a thirty-five-year wine marketing career. After moving to Varenna in 2019, she joined the Writers Club and

has served as editor of *The Villaggio*, Varenna's resident newsletter.

Loreen Barry was born in New York City, grew up in Washington D.C., received her B.A. from the University of Maryland, and her MLA from Johns Hopkins University. She has lived in Baltimore, MD; San Juan, Puerto Rico; Summit, NJ; McLean, VA; Plant City, FL; and for the past 27 years, Santa Rosa. While her main focus has been the Visual Arts, she feels that the Writers Club has helped her to better express herself verbally.

Susan Bono, Editor, is an editor and writing teacher living in Petaluma. She edited and published *Tiny Lights: A Journal of Personal Narrative* from 1995-2015 and edited the *Noyo River Review* for eight years. Her writing has appeared in print, online, on stage, and on the radio. Her book of collected essays is *What Have We Here: Essays about Keeping House and Finding Home.*

Myrna Graves Fleckles was born and reared in Southern California until she was twelve, when she and her parents moved to San Francisco. She earned her A.B. degree and teaching credential at Stanford and completed her M.A. in counseling and administration at SF State. After a 42-year career in both K-12 and State University systems, she volunteered for various community groups. She's been married for over fifty years to David, who has shared her enthusiasm for her career and community involvements. They moved to Varenna from San Jose in 2011. The Writers Club is her favorite activity at Varenna.

Vicki Frink, a life-long Maryland resident, recently located with her husband Jack to California at the insistence of their daughter. Initially skeptical of the whole laid-back, hyper-friendly lifestyle portrayed on television, she discovered she was fulfilling her destiny and now self-identifies as a Northern Californian. She now greets any and all passers-by cheerfully, composts, rejoices in every raindrop, and loves foggy mornings followed by sunny afternoons.

Ina Green was born in The Bronx. She's the proud product of the New York City School System, a graduate of the High School of Music and Art (piano major) and of Hunter College (speech therapy.) She also attended the Juilliard School of Music. A love of Gilbert and Sullivan operettas brought her a short career in amateur productions in New York and New Jersey.

Ina and Alfred were married in 1955. Their four children gave them six grandchildren. At the invitation of the California kids, Al and Ina became Californians in 2020 and Varenna residents in 2021. Ina enjoys the Writers Club. She dedicates her offerings here to Al's memory.

Nancy Humphriss grew up in Northampton, Massachusetts. After graduating from the University of Massachusetts, she married her hometown sweetheart, raised a family, and followed her husband to seven different states, Sydney, Australia, and Jerusalem. Her teaching career began with first graders in Florida. After earning her master's degree in Comparative Literature from Indiana University, Nancy ended her career teaching foreign students for 17 years at San Jose State University. She and her husband retired to Santa Rosa in 1997 and moved to Varenna in 2009. She feels very fortunate to have had such a satisfying life.

Nikki King, born and raised in Fargo, North Dakota, received her B.A. from Mills College in Oakland, California. After graduation, she moved to San Francisco and married a student from USF Law School. She and her husband (a retired Justice) have one son and have been married for over sixty years. At forty-nine, she attended graduate school, got a master's in counseling, and was a psychotherapist for eleven years. In her years at Varenna, Nikki has begun to reflect on her life experiences and write brief memoirs about incidents that stand out in her mind.

Nancy Parsons was born in a small town in central Pennsylvania, studied nursing in Philadelphia, and eventually moved to San Francisco to find adventure and soak up the joys of California living. Just before "the Summer of Love," she married Gerry and moved to Marin County where they raised their two children. After a career in nursing, she earned her B.A. in Humanities from Dominican College just before she started collecting social security. Nancy loves traveling, gardening, playing Rummikub, her granddaughters, meeting people, making friends, and sharing adventures, which makes Varenna the perfect place for her and husband, Henk, to call home.

Hal Peters spent his first eleven years in the Sacramento Valley as the son of a sheep rancher in a town with a population of 1,100. When his parents divorced, he moved with his mother to Marin County, where he lived until 1962. That's when he, his wife, and son settled in Orange County, and he began his career as a manufacturer's agent for sporting goods and sportswear manufacturers. In 1990, he retired to Monterey County until 2006, when he came to Santa Rosa. As a high school English major, he especially enjoyed essay composition and is delighted to reintroduce himself to the craft as a member of the Varenna Writers Club.

In 1998 **Carole Williams** and her husband, Richard, retired to Napa Valley, escaping the harsh New York winters and blazing summers. They loved their years in St Helena, but the time came when they needed all that Assisted Living offers. It was hard to switch valleys, but they made the right decision. Carole got involved in a lot of Varenna activities but avoided the Writing Class for three years. She'd done a lot of writing as a Psychoanalyst, but creative writing was anathema. Eventually someone persuaded her to try a class, and she was hooked. The group is fun (truth be told, she goes for the laughs), the instructor is consistently supportive, kind, and helpful, and Carole is happy to have stories to pass on.

Hildy Williams is a retired Marriage, Child and Family Therapist who has lived in Sonoma County since 1980. Hildy was originally from Los Angeles where she attended school. She earned her master's degree from USC. Hildy has two children and three grandchildren. She enjoys spending time with the kids, thrifting, exercising, and can now add writing to this list.

 **Geoff Withrington** grew up in London's East End. He studied electrical engineering at the University of Leeds. After marrying Shirley in 1966, he joined a startup company, travelling to the USA to start a new subsidiary, then on to Japan with two boys, ages three months and eighteen months, to do the same there. He returned to England three years later as CEO of the company. After Geoff's early retirement in 1998, he and Shirley purchased a 40-foot yacht and learned to sail. They spent ten years sailing the Mediterranean, visiting virtually every country bordering that sea. They came to Varenna in 2018.

I'll tell you a secret. Old Storytellers never die. They disappear into their own story.

Vera Nazarian

Made in the USA
Middletown, DE
08 November 2023

42137437R00104